Theaker's Quarterly Fiction #52

Edited by
Stephen Theaker
and John Greenwood

Other titles from this publisher and related entities

SPACE UNIVERSITY TRENT: HYPERPARASITE
Walt Brunston

THEAKER'S QUARTERLY FICTION #1–51
Stephen Theaker and John Greenwood (eds)

THERE ARE NOW A BILLION FLOWERS
THE HATCHLING (FORTHCOMING)
John Greenwood

THE MERCURY ANNUAL
PILGRIMS AT THE WHITE HORIZON
Michael Wyndham Thomas

THE CONAN DOYLE WEIRDBOOK
Rafe McGregor (ed.)

PROFESSOR CHALLENGER IN SPACE
QUIET, THE TIN CAN BRAINS ARE HUNTING!
THE FEAR MAN
HOWARD PHILLIPS IN HIS NERVES EXTRUDED
HOWARD PHILLIPS AND THE DOOM THAT CAME TO SEA BASE DELTA
HOWARD PHILLIPS AND THE DAY THE MOON WEPT BLOOD
Stephen Theaker

FIVE FORGOTTEN STORIES
John Hall

ELEPHANT
Harsh Grewal

ELSEWHERE
Steven Gilligan

NEW WORDS #1–4
John Greenwood, Steven Gilligan and Stephen Theaker (eds)

Theaker's Quarterly Fiction #52

Edited by
Stephen Theaker
and John Greenwood

Cover Artist

Howard Watts

Contributors

Len Saculla
Yarrow Paisley
Jacob Edwards
Walt Brunston
Howard Phillips
Douglas J. Ogurek

ISBN (print): 978-1-910387-09-2
ISBN (epub): 978-1-910387-10-8

ISSN (print): 1747-6083
ISSN (online): 1747-6075

Website: www.theakersquarterly.blogspot.com

Email: theakersquarterlyfiction@gmail.com

Lulu Store: www.lulu.com/silveragebooks

Feedbooks: www.feedbooks.com/userbooks/tag/tqf

Submissions: Submissions are very welcome! See website for guidelines and terms.

Advertising: We welcome ad swaps with small press publishers and other creative types, and we'll run ads for relevant new projects from former contributors.

Sending material for review: We are interested in reviewing almost anything that's fantasy-related. We prefer to receive books for review in epub or mobi format. Feel free to send ebooks without querying first. We have reviewed about 14% of items received, though many of those reviewed are things we've actively requested.

Mission statement: The primary goal of *Theaker's Quarterly Fiction* is to keep going. If you're wondering why we do something a particular way, our primary goal is probably why.

Published in Theaker's Paperback Library on 14 August 2015.

Contents

Editorial

Fiction

The Quarterly Review

*Reviews by Douglas J. Ogurek, Stephen Theaker
and Jacob Edwards*

Audio

Books

Editorial

Stephen Theaker

Short reviews

In the last couple of issues, as a bit of an experiment, our normal reviews have been complemented by a bunch of short notes at the back about everything else I've been reading. It's been working out well for me, so in this issue the notes have been promoted to being part of the proper review sections.

I wouldn't go so far as to call them reviews yet, just because I have an idea about what a review should be, and what it should try to do, that it should try to contain the entire book within itself, and look at it from various angles, and that's not what I'm doing with these. I'm bashing out whatever pops into my head, and if I don't have anything to say about the book, I'm not fretting about it. If pressed, I'd still call them notes rather than reviews.

On the other hand, I do feel to some extent that a star rating is the purest form of review. A controversial point of view, but for me there's no way to spin a star rating, to skip over your misgivings and dance around the flaws, it just says outright how good you thought it was.

There are a few benefits of taking this approach. One is that my freelance work is going well at the moment, so it's increasingly tricky to find a half day spare to write a full-length review, but I can find fifteen minutes to write a short note or review every day of the week.

Another is that I read a lot of books, so if I write a short review of all of them that adds up to lots of pages for the zine, even if each review is shorter.

It also encourages me to read more books and comics and listen to more audios that are sent in for review, because I won't be adding extra jobs to my to-do list that I don't realistically have time to do.

I'll also be able to write the reviews right after reading something, instead of waiting and waiting for the right moment, and then having to read the whole thing again because it was so long ago that I've forgotten it!

I'm hoping though that as I keep writing these short notes that my reviewing muscles, which had grown rather weak over the last year or so, will build up again. I'm happy with the reviews I wrote over that time, but by gum I had to put a lot of time into them! I want to write more naturally, rather than painstakingly stitching together reviews over days and weeks. With luck the short notes will get better, and eventually reach the point where I'm happy to call them reviews.

Biographies

Another slight change in this issue: the contributor biographies now appear at the bottom of their stories rather than here in the editorial. Hope you don't mind, but let me know if you do: it's just to let me get more of the issue finished in advance, and so the contributors can check their bios on the proofs along with everything else, without me having to run off a separate pdf of the contributors section.

Guest editor for issue 54

We will have a guest editor for issue 54, our Christmas issue: our cover artist Howard Watts, and he is looking for submissions on a special theme! Take it away, Howard:

Calling all contributors!

Take a look at the back cover of this issue. What's going on with these three characters? Their fate lies in your hands! TQF is looking for short stories based on this image, to appear in issue 54, guest edited by me, Howard Watts. Normal TQF guidelines will apply, but I'm looking for strong character, conflict and ultimately plot – a completely developed idea, with a resolution.

The shortlisted stories will be published in the zine, and an online poll will then ask the readership to decide the most popular. The author of that story will receive a year's subscription to TQF (or a cash equivalent if outside the UK) and a large jpeg version of the art, with a white border with their story title beneath it – suitable for framing by one of the many high street photographic shops or online art sites, such as Snapfish.

Submissions to: **howardsw@sky.com**
Deadline: **31 October 2015**

Stephen Theaker's reviews have appeared in Black Static, Interzone, Prism and the BFS Journal, as well as clogging up our pages. He shares his home with three slightly smaller Theakers, runs the British Fantasy Awards, and works in legal and medical publishing.

Rocking Horse Traffic

Yarrow Paisley

I awoke from my usual dream (rocking horse traffic) to find my father's hands fiddling inside my stomach.

"Just making an adjustment," he assured me, but I felt uneasy all the same. I had been aware of nothing amiss, nothing needing adjustment... and usually, my father informed me in advance of these operations.

My head sought comfort from my fluffy pillow, and I submitted to his ministrations placidly. I was accustomed to this pain... I "stepped aside" and revived highlights of my dream to pass the time. The horses' eyes were black, and their teeth were white, or possibly the reverse.

After a few minutes, my father carefully sewed my belly up and said, "Okay, good morning, Bobby!"

Grinning, his forelock wayward, he bent to kiss my brow; the pleasant, foamy mist of his breath diffused over my face and warmed me back into my body.

"Hungry for breakfast?"

I wasn't hungry, but I nodded, my assent habitual to my father's queries. It's not that I don't dare to disagree with him, but only that I can't see why I should.

My somber mien, perhaps, elicited a smile from my father, and he ruffled my hair. I always giggle when he does this – it is one of our rituals of affection – but this time, I failed.

Instead, I coughed and felt some wetness on my lower lip.

My father, squinting at me, frowned and said, "Shit."

He wiped my mouth with his smooth finger, and I glimpsed the familiar dark goo of my blood upon its tip as he hastily withdrew it.

"Well," he said, rubbing the finger clean on his cotton smock, "Well... hum... After breakfast, Bobby. Just a little adjustment, that's all. We'll have you fixed up, let's just see what breakfast does, okay?"

I made to gather my strength to heave myself from bed, but my father scooped me up and carried me into the kitchen in the baby way. I enjoyed the ride, feeling weightless yet secure pressed up against his manly chest, although the faint, coppery scent of my bloodstain on his smock instilled me with a touch of nausea.

I had been doing well the last week or so. My limbs had been strengthening, my muscles building and stretching, my lungs swelling to a new capacity. I had played on the playground... the slide, the swings, even the merry-go-round... I had "frolicked", as my father bade me do, my breath become an exhilarating wind streaming through me, my body a trumpet blown triumphantly.

This morning, however, I felt strange again, and weak... listless... like before. I considered revealing these symptoms to my father, but I didn't want to disappoint him.

It's okay, I thought, *we'll wait to see what breakfast does.*

My father sprinkled walnuts and raisins on my cereal. I don't like them, but I didn't protest. I was hardly strong enough to lift the spoon up to my mouth, or even to grind the food between my molars.

He sat across the table, watching me eat. I pointed with my spoon to his barren placemat, and he waved his hand dismissively. "I already had mine," he said, but I knew that was not true. He always brushed his teeth after a meal, yet there had been no spearmint on his breath.

My bowl emptied only by half, I set my spoon down and hung my head. My father came around and knelt by my chair. His arms wrapped around me and drew me close. His cheek and nose were cool in my neck.

"It's okay, just eat what you can."

His voice's thrum became my flesh.

"I love you, Bobby."

My seam throbbed.

"Let's see what we've got, huh?"

He lifted me up and took me into the bathroom, setting me on my feet in front of the toilet. I steeled myself not to "step aside" this time: I couldn't poop without my spirit.

Afraid to split my belly's fresh stitches by bending, I made magic motions with my hands that compelled my father to pull down my pajamas for me. Upon exposure, my pecker immediately squirted a limpid stream onto his smock. I backed myself onto the toilet-seat and began to cry.

My father made a cooing noise deep in his chest, his customary mode of consolation, and he ruffled my hair, but my crying increased. Weakness flurried down my ribs in nauseating waves. Something was strange and wrong inside of me.

"Just give it a shot," he murmured.

I gave it a shot – filling my lungs, straightening my spine, and contracting all my muscles in the way my father'd taught me. As I strained, a blade of pain sliced rhythmically down my torso, whimsically hacking at my organs. I could not sustain the effort, and I relaxed, leaning back against the tank as I gasped for breath.

"Anything?" my father asked, peering avidly between my legs. I spread them apart to improve his view, but I knew, without looking, that the water would be clear.

My father emitted a frustrated sigh. "What, what... maybe the kefir? Let's try that, what do you think?"

I found myself too weak to respond in any manner, save a few blinks. My father kissed the top of my head and said, "I'll be right back, Bobby. I've got the flavoured kind, you'll love it."

When my father was gone, my mother "stepped in". Her eyes were round, as though frightened, but that was just an illusion stemming from the spiritual effect: her smile, genuine, was radiant with her love, and she waved to me.

I could not wave back; I could not move.

Her smile increased – she was always keen to encounter me when I could not afford resistance – and she reached for my hands, commenced to guide them toward my belly. I tried to shake my head and to pull my arms away, but in my weakened condition, no movements were possible for me, other than those my mother directed.

I could not "step aside", since my mother's grasp was immitigable, and so, for the moment, I had to endure the agony. My mother used my fingernails to slice the criss-cross threads and speared my fingers deep into the peeling seam... establishing a grip upon the flaps... followed by a heaving wrench that opened me up... and out spilled my slimy tubes, unfurling everywhere – draped across my legs, piled up on the floor, and even slithering down between my thighs to fill the toilet-bowl.

Once she was satisfied that I was inside-out and dead, my mother released her grip so that she could grab for my second body, the one I employed to "step aside"... as ever, she wanted me to "step out", in order to be with her, but I am an agile boy in some respects: I "stepped aside" just in time, away from her reach, and I found myself among the horses.

Far away, I could hear my mother scream her rage

and sorrow. As her long shrieks faded, I began also to hear my father's wails. Unable to resist my curiosity, I peeked.

In the bathtub lay a discarded bottle of kefir, its maroon and viscous contents – a raspberry flavour, perhaps, which I'm sure I would have enjoyed – glugging languorously out of the neck into a thick, expanding pool.

My father, frantically, was gathering up my numerous and lengthy tubes from the floor and toilet-bowl. His tears splashed all over them as he stuffed them into an oily trash bag.

My mother had fled. She preferred to keep her distance from my father.

With the bag in one hand and my limp body slung over his opposite shoulder, my father hurried out of the bathroom and rushed toward the surgical theatre he maintained in the garage. I left him to his duty, trusting him to fix me up – he never failed in this task. Never.

To pass the time, I entertained myself among the horses. Some were on rockers, some sustained on poles, others balanced on their prancing feet. Their jowls were sudsy, but not wet, no... rather, a sculptural froth.

Indeed, everything about them was sculptural... the wind-shaped manes, the bulging, frenzied eyes, the realistic sweat drops on their muscular haunches... and painted... so many variant hues, yet combined without discord... without exception, these mystical colours glowing outward in accordance with a harmonious principle.

A silence reigned, as was usual in this spiritual world. But no, a susurration seemed manifest, a gentle rhythm upon my senses... so it was a breathing silence.

I sensed in this "breathing silence" a plenitude of tides and forces... measureless activity... conversations among men and spirits... creatures historical and mythical... material and oneiric... an endless parade of characters and events. The choices so profuse, I could attend to none of them; yet I chided myself for my confusion, my constructed retreat into this typical dream of rocking horse traffic.

It struck me that a particular horse appealed to me more than the others. Unlike them, its eyes were shut, concealing from me the frightening, manic stare that characterised all the sculpted beasts in this region. Its dappled hide was pleasing – brown and white with flecks of redness – and the smooth, worn saddle upon its back invited me to sit there.

I mounted up, and held the reins with a ginger care. I am not practised in the riding of horses; I had never dared before to stride one, only to wander among them and occasionally stroke their hard, cool skin. Not knowing what else to do, I commenced to rocking... and the silence of the world scampered into hiding... chased away by the slow creak of my steed's rockers.

As if powered by the energy of my "trot", the world around me began to roll by. What before had been a blank screen transformed into a movie.

Stars blinkered in and wheeled about on multiple axes. Continents floated on oceans of liquefied rock. I saw multitudes of people swarming on the landscapes, and within their brains were other swarms, and within their bodies infestations... scarabs scuttling through the pipes... spiders with a hundred eyes, all useless in the dark... and babies, so many human babies, defective in their manufacture, curled into balls and ready for disposal. And so much more – all possible forms of disease, invasion, squalor, and somatic decrepitude.

Then, the movie settled into a story, for which the preceding montage had merely served as prelude.

I saw a surgical theatre, the very one in my father's garage. I saw my father and my mother, both embodied, both alive... my mother alive... embodied... the idea had never occurred to me.

My living mother was laid out on the table – so familiar to me from my own numerous operations and adjustments – her limbs strapped down, her chest sawn open and, within that cavity, her lumpen heart exposed and quivering with its living pulses.

My father bent over her, performing adjustments in the meat with gleamy instruments, his concentration as intense as I had ever seen it. My mother was asleep, and yet soon evoked to wakefulness by the sound of a weakly keening voice – my own voice, I realised.

My keening voice, but not mine, no... a baby's voice.

I spurred my rocking horse beyond its creaking gait, impelled it to a gallop's pace, and the film sped up commensurately.

My mother's head ratcheted from side to side, her eyeballs spinning frantically, searching for the source of her child's cries. I saw, from my vantage, that the baby mewled in its playpen... my playpen... my... my cries incited by a ragged suture in my neck that had been torn by contact with an exposed velcro strap in the playpen's netted siding.

My mother could not locate me. From my present saddle, I attempted to speak to her, to inform her, but I could not speak, not in this... body.

Not from this mount, not from this dream, not from this time.

What I saw could not be altered; it was a scene drawn from the world's memory, a fixed image, upon which I could only gaze and seek to store it in my own memory.

My revery had slowed me near to stillness, and the

actors on the screen now moved with excruciating care as in a cinematic scene of slow-motion catastrophe.

My father set his hand upon my mother's shoulder to steady her. "Liiinnnnddddaaa," he said, "Caaaalllmmmm yooourrrrsssseeeeeellfff."

I spurred my steed into a canter. I yearned for speed, but also wished for time to observe the details.

My father strapped my mother's head to still her struggles, and he caressed the perspiration from her brow and cheeks. "It's okay, honey," he said, infusing his voice with cheer, although his expression was worried and ghastly with exhaustion. "Bobby's just had a little accident. I'll have him fixed up in a jiffy, and then we'll put the finishings on your repairs. Shouldn't be much longer."

He limped over to the playpen and lifted out the baby, a soothing lullaby humming from his chest. Gently, he placed me on the changing table and began to inspect the damaged stitch.

Meanwhile, my mother's fingers curled inward and prodded at the strap that bound her wrist. Slowly, carefully, she managed to loosen the velcro's grip until her wrist was freed. Then she freed her head and her other limbs.

When she stood up, her heart slipped out of its station and dangled down her sternum. Although she tried, she could not stifle her agony's croak. My father turned and cried out.

"No, Linda! Get back on there!"

My mother cradled her heart in her hands and swayed. Her voice a hoarse whisper, she said, "It's all a shambles, John, it's no good."

My father shook his head placatingly, but his eyes betrayed a desperate sheen. "Lie back down, it'll be all right, I swear." He lifted up the baby and made to return me to the playpen. "Just lie down, honey, and

I'll have that fixed up in time for dinner. You know me."

"I do, I do, John, and I love you, and I love Bobby, too." With that, her jaw opened wide, and she took a bite from what she held.

Before he could reach her, she had already chewed and swallowed half the muscle. Wailing, my father tried to fix it up, but he simply didn't have the materials.

I awoke from this dream to find myself upon the operating table. My father leaned over me, his smile resurgent and relieved.

"All better now, Bobby, that was a close call."

I peered down and saw that my belly was sewn back up. I tensed my muscles, attempting to sense the presence of my organs, and a small, gray loop of intestine poked out between two sutures.

My father flinched and said, "Oops. Hum, well, that's not a problem." He took up his scalpel and flicked at the surrounding stitches, then pried apart the flaps to gain access to the errant organ.

I opened and shut my mouth a few times for practice, licked my lips, and said, "Daddy." My throat burned with the unaccustomed speech, and my father paused his work to look at me, amazed.

"Yes... Bobby?"

"What happened to my mother?"

He scowled and shook his head with annoyance, but then his features assumed a more sorrowful shape, and he sighed. "No point dwelling there, Bobby. No point at all." His eyes met mine and softened, then shifted away again. "There's nothing... can't be fixed."

"Daddy," I whispered. "I love you, Daddy."

My father looked surprised and grateful, even jubilant – then suddenly bewildered as I took the scalpel from his unwary fingers and drew it across his throat. His hot blood rained upon me, soon filling all the spaces in my opened belly, and we both relaxed into a torporous pose.

Together, then, at long last and hand-in-hand, we "stepped out" to join you, Mother.

Yarrow Paisley lives in the Pioneer Valley of Western Massachusetts, USA. His fiction has appeared in Shimmer, Strange Tales V (Tartarus Press), Sein und Werden, and Dadaoism: An Anthology (Chômu Press), among others.

Quest for Lost Beauty

A Dim Star Is Born, Part 3

Howard Phillips

From that moment my only thought was to find Pierre Samuel. All else in my life was forgotten. Meaningless. Was it love? Obsession? Infatuation? The foolishness of a middle-aged poet? All of them, most likely. Or none. I don't know any more. Those days seem so long ago, my memories shrouded in the ashen rags of the events that came later.

I went to every gathering of poets I could find. Endless interminable readings, where the fixed smile on my face wore hard as buffoons declaimed their idiotic doggerel. Poetry slams that were more like gentle shoves. Book launches where the authors of six-poem pamphlets were treated like gods. I went to them all, queued for signed copies, asked questions to show that I (I alone, in most cases) had been listening.

All in hopes of meeting Pierre Samuel.

And month after month my hopes came to nothing. As the recycling bin swelled heavy with the leavings of my search I refused to give up. He was out there. We would meet.

If he had escaped assassination.

As far as I knew, I had assured his safety, but what if others were sent? And who would be doing the sending? The beautiful attract enemies simply by existing. I know this myself, being cursed with a winsome gauntness that often appeals to the melancholic type. If I did not find him, perhaps someone else would first, and that lent urgency to my quest.

I did of course try the more usual avenues of discovery. I couldn't simply post on Twitter and ask if anyone knew him; if I had any hopes of ever developing my relationship with him, that would seem unforgivably gauche; and if someone were to answer his enemies might see that answer too. Or he might think me one of them, and disappear forever! It could not be risked. But I did search in ways that could not be traced or tracked: I searched telephone directories, went through back issues of poetry journals, tried to find copies of his work (which were unaccountably scarce – someone must do something about that, I thought to myself at the time).

Nothing came of it. No one mentioned him, no one published him, no one grabbed my arm and said, "Have you seen Pierre Samuel? He's gorgeous!"

But then, one day, a day in February, I was browsing a secondhand bookshop in Reading, looking for a present for Theaker's upcoming birthday (I make a happy point of presenting him with poetry in print books whenever the occasion requires an offering, knowing he dislikes both ingredients in that cake), when I bumped elbows with someone browsing the same shelves.

I made no attempt to keep irritation from my face as I turned to face this inconsiderate jostler, but it melted away as I saw who it was. Pierre Samuel. In the flesh. The golden, downy flesh. In a tight blue Star Trek t-shirt that outlined the contours of his body as if it worked for the Ordnance Survey.

"It wasn't my fault," he said, which was a relief since

it makes it so much harder to write these stories when no one talks to each other. "That guy over there banged into me."

I nodded. Of course he could never have done anything wrong. He was far too lovely. And I was far too lonely. Perhaps if I had still been in touch with my old friends from the Saturation Point I would not have been so vulnerable to his charms. What if? The question that haunts our lives. Though in this case there is no need to ask it. I lived the "if". The question is rather, what if not? Would my life have been better? Would I now be happier? Wait till the end and see what you think.

"I understand," I said, though there was no "guy" to be seen. And I wasn't looking anyway.

He nodded, and that would have been the end of the encounter had I not leapt upon the opportunity like a cat upon a miniaturised human.

"You are a poet, are you not?" asked this silly lovelorn fool.

"I am, that's right," he said. "I think everyone is. Everyone should follow their heart, and ignore those who tell them otherwise. A poet's job is to spread this message to the world."

I put a hand on his shoulder. "I could not agree more," I said. "It is exactly what I think about poetry." And as of that moment it was. "You're Pierre Samuel, aren't you?"

He tilted his head and frowned. "That's right. I'm sorry, I don't know you."

That was odd, given my worldwide fame at the height of the Saturation Point's musical celebrity, but I paid it no mind. Not then, at least.

"I am Howard Phillips," I said with a slight bow.

"Well, pleased to meet you," he said. The name obviously meant nothing to him whatsoever, and he was clearly now ready to disengage himself from the conversation.

I understood, of course. Personally, I have never spoken to a person in my life without thinking that they would rather be speaking to someone else, and so I have a habit of cutting conversations abruptly short. This causes other people to assume I don't like them, whereas the truth is that I assume they won't like me and so make haste to leave them alone.

But I was not ready to leave *this* conversation. A man's life was at stake. The lives of two men, perhaps.

"Look," I said, doing everything I could physically to stop him leaving, short of actually grabbing his arm. "This may seem strange, but I have been searching for you for the last month."

Alarm flashed upon his beautiful face. He drew back in horror and prepared to run, which wouldn't be easy among those shelves overflowing with paperbacks.

"Don't go," I said. "I'm a friend, truly." He relaxed a little, but was still wary. "I saw your photograph, in January."

"Where?" he asked. "I do my best to keep away from cameras. Beauty is in the eye of the beholder, not the lens of a camera."

"I could not agree more," I declared, busily beholding. "The source of the photograph is what I wanted to talk to you about."

He toyed with a copy of an *Ultramarines* omnibus by Graham McNeil. The cover showed futuristic soldiers in blue armour fighting for their lives. I knew how they felt. If Pierre Samuels were to flee now all would be lost. The book, according to the cover quote, featured "great characters, truck loads of intrigue and an amazing sense of pace". How that resonated in that moment! I was with a great character, he intrigued me, and I hoped things would move at pace.

"Have you read it?" I asked, trying to relax him a bit.

"Yes, of course," he said without emotion, "I always hunt in second-hand bookshops for books I've already read. And my favourite thing to read is *of course* Warhammer 40,000 tie-in novels."

I couldn't tell if he was being sarcastic or serious. I chose to say nothing rather than say something foolish. At least he wasn't leaving. He was so lovely to look at, like syrup sponge and custard for the eyes. I wanted to tell him, but couldn't. I had been with men before, naturally, but this was different. This time I actually cared.

"I don't actually believe in reading," he continued. "It's so twentieth century." I nodded in utter agreement. "Books are for yesterday's men. Poetry cannot live but from a living speaker. Without that it is dead and worthless."

"So wise..." I shook my head and pulled myself together. Gazing into his eyes was pleasant, but would not serve my cause. "And the subject of living poets is exactly why we must talk. Your life is in danger."

He nodded.

"That doesn't seem to be a surprise," I observed.

He shrugged. "Everyone has haters. Especially beautiful blondes like myself."

"This is rather more than that," I said with some concern. "These are murderous maniacs with their teeth filed into points, stalking the streets of London with your photograph in their pockets."

"Jealous rivals, I expect."

"They had a secret base. I destroyed it for you."

He smiled as if to say I needn't have bothered and he owed me nothing for it.

"Could we go for a cup of tea, talk it over?"

"I don't think so." He held up his hand. There was a golden band upon his ring finger. "I'm married, Harold. And you aren't my type."

He put the book down and ambled towards the exit. I sank into myself in sorrow. It was over. I wouldn't become a stalker. I would respect his wishes and leave him alone. And die, slowly, of unhappiness. I would waste away to nothing.

But then the bookseller, a doughty old fellow with a pipe hanging from his mouth, came to my rescue. From beneath his desk he pulled out a weapon. Seventy centimetres long, flashing from one end to the other, and sitting in his fists like a stick of dynamite with a grudge. He pointed it at Pierre and gave it a squeeze.

Five bookcases exploded into a shower of paper shreds, but Pierre had scrambled clear. He was still too far from the exit to escape, and now the gun was trained upon him and there was nowhere else to scramble to.

My turn to shine. I picked up the Ultramarines book – it seemed appropriate – and ran at the "bookseller" – swinging it above my head and screaming like a banshee. It startled the bookseller long enough for me to reach him, and I clobbered him about the head with the book, all seven hundred and sixty-eight pages of it. He was soon unconscious, and I jumped up and down on his gun until it was broken.

"Now will you listen?" I asked Pierre.

He shrugged. "If I must."

Howard Phillips is a dissolute poet whose previous contribution to this zine received such bad reviews that he wept for three days, burned seventeen unpublished novels, and wrote a series of angry blog posts accusing various parties of disparaging his genius. We asked him why he had taken it so badly, and he replied, "If you need to ask, you'll never know."

Zom-Boyz Have All the Luck

Len Saculla

Music and drugs. The two had probably gone together since the first shaman ate some dodgy fungus and was inspired to chant and bang some sticks together. Spin the clock forward and every type of music had some sort of mind or mood altering chemical attached to it, from tavern songs through psychedelic pop to Ecstasy culture and beyond. The difference this time was that a group with teen appeal was being so open about their use of semi-legal substances.

"The thing is," Roddy explained, "our fans are so devoted that they want to experience our music in full. A tab of Zombol allows them to do that."

The interviewer screwed up her pretty nose and responded, "Don't you think that you are simply encouraging your fans – mostly teenage girls, let's be honest – to become addicted."

Roddy put on his best boyish smile, hoping it might work to charm both the presenter and the watching millions. "No one forces anyone to do anything. That's what we're all about here – personal freedom. Away from the yoke of your parents, school, peer pressure, everything. If our followers want to get deeper into the music and if Zombol helps them, surely that's not a bad thing?"

The presenter flicked her bobbed brown head away

from him, beamed at the camera, "Roddy from the Zom-Boyz there; spokesman for a generation. We'll be back after a quick word from our sponsors – Carlsberg Breweries."

Roddy and the taciturn bass player Glen were shuffled away from the studio straight away so he never got the chance to try his luck with Sally Churchill. Ah well, there would be plenty of blissed out Zom-girls at the gig tonight.

Patterson was in his face as he reached the dressing room. "Good job there, son," the tough, Scottish-born manager buzzed. "Keep us in the headlines."

Roddy shrugged. "For all the wrong reasons, by the sounds of it. We never even got to show a clip from our video."

"Don't matter, kid. There are no wrong reasons. Only stories, items and features. Come on, the tour bus is waiting."

Half an hour till show-time. Patterson was prowling round the backstage area of White Mount Arena, making sure that none of his protégés was sipping too much Jack Daniel's or snorting any white powders. So much for do what you want and be down with the free music. Roddy was checking messages on his smartphone until Patterson came along and confiscated it.

"Concentrate on the show, son. Let me deal with the real world, eh?"

Roddy shook his head, gently tuned up his guitar, strummed the D major to G major opening of "Love Me Like a Zombie". Billy tapped his knees in a rhythm that was too fast. Hopefully he would keep his headphones with the click track firmly on tonight.

The screams were welling up from the mosh pit. Patterson called Clyde, head of security, over and handed him a large bin bag full of pills. "Let's zone those mothers out," he ordered.

"I doubt that many of them are mothers," Roddy quipped but Patterson simply glared in his direction. The manager had told him twice this week that no one was irreplaceable. Roddy hoped that might be true about managers also.

Roddy always steeled himself to simply get through the first two songs. The band played a couple of the million download numbers that had made their name, battling against the high-pitched bat-like squeaking and screaming of their adoring public. By the end of their third number, however, a magical change came across the crowd as the Rohypnol derivatives handed out with the Pepsi colas began to take effect. A comparative hush and stillness settled like a palpable cloud over the audience.

"Any musos in the crowd," Roddy spat into the microphone, "now's your time to listen and know that we can really play."

He launched into the descending guitar figure that indicated the opening of "Love is Like a Stone in My Heart" and the crowd swayed in unison like a field of tall grain in a southern breeze. The crew swept searchlights across the punters – white, yellow, blue. Glen settled into his hypnotic bass loop and Billy opened and closed his arms like they were the jaws of a giant cetacean, brushing the cymbals and caressing the snare.

Roddy gazed out at the listeners now revealed to him. It was the usual crowd: girls and young women with kohl-set eye sockets; their skin painted alabaster whatever its natural coloration once was; their mostly bare, tattoo-free arms gradually rising in front of their bodies as if reaching out towards the electrified energy

emanated by the band. The Zom-Boyz were the focus...
the source... the target.

Roddy had played guitar since he was seven and
been busking outside clubs and bars since the age of
twelve but he had never quite dreamed of having this
control, of holding thousands of people in thrall to his
every gentle note.

Of course, it was mostly the drugs, the Zombol
tablets that their hardcore fans ate like Smarties. But it
was partly the music, too. You couldn't have one
without the other. Hypnotic. Brain-mashing.

When the epic song finally finished, there was a
collective exhalation of held breath almost strong
enough to knock him off his Caterpillar booted feet.
He didn't bother to introduce the next song, just
nodded over at his band mates to slip into their
groove. As his plectrum descended, a loving groan
emerged from the front rows. As one they began to
push towards the empty buffer zone, trying to clamber
over the fencing and pushing at the security staff with
surprising strength and determination.

Roddy left the last note hanging, briefly held his
Fender aloft and quit the stage. The Zom-Boyz didn't
do encores.

He was escorted to the tour bus. Donaldson, the
driver, had the engine running but was under strict
instructions not to set off until the band had picked
up companions for the night. After about five minutes,
the first gaggle of females stumbled their way into the
car park, arms still outstretched and eyes glazed. Their
mouths moved up and down like expiring fish. One
could make out the low, longing cry of *"Zom-Boyz!
Zom-Boyz!"* even though lips and words didn't seem to
be entirely in sync. Patterson ushered the first five into
the vehicle, their white-painted flesh and vacant
expressions made all the more shocking by the interior
lights which blazed for thirty seconds after the door

opened.

"Let's quit this dead town, guys," the manager muttered.

Roddy had a small torch in his left hand. It was the one he used to tune up on stage when the band were playing in cavernous darkness. He could have found his confiscated phone in Patterson's jacket just by feel, though. He flicked one device off and the other on; went straight to a rolling newsfeed. Things were looking pretty bleak right across the world as the plague was starting to hit. Everyone had breathed a sigh of relief a week or so ago when it seemed that this would just be a minor ailment; clearly, it was all to do with a longer than usual period of incubation. And here we are fiddling while Rome burns, or whatever the expression is, Roddy mused.

A low noise from behind him distracted his attention from the screen. It was the girl he'd chosen – Kerry, Kirsty, Chloe, whatever she'd said. She wasn't actually speaking, just uttering guttural demands that he return to his bunk and see to her needs again. She had a cute ass, smooth white legs and arms, but her eyes were still glazed from the Zombol and he wondered once again how much it was her desire imploring him and how much it was simply an effect of the semi-legal brain suppressant. He realized, not for the first time, that he slightly despised the band's fans. Manipulated, mind-dead motherfuckers the lot of them. Nubile and available, which was not to be sniffed at, but at base they were stupid automatons with no true free will.

He resolved to write a song about them. Smart enough and metaphorical enough to not be too obvious, though.

He let her hands grasp him. Her mouth was opening and closing like a catfish.

They made a morning stop at a one-horse town with no visible horses, paid off the groupies with sufficient cash for a cab fare back to wherever they belonged. As the tour bus pulled away, Roddy noticed that the girls' body make-up was starting to streak and at least two of the girls were revealed to be of African-American heritage. And yet they wanted to be deathly white. They'd do absolutely anything to become Zom-Girlz. *Had* done absolutely anything to attain that status.

There was some problem at the next large town. Police cars, painted white and black like monochrome predators, blocked the road and the band's manager Patterson finally started to earn his corn. The negotiations continued for the best part of an hour. Quiet Glen spent most of the time on the chemical toilet evacuating his queasy bowels. One of the younger guys in the road crew might have to deputize for him at the show tonight. If there was a show tonight...

Billy had been prowling up and down the aisle of the lower deck like a caged cheetah. Finally he could stand it no more and went outside to join the impromptu conference.

Roddy curled himself up into the confines of his bunk, strummed a few chords that might go into a new composition. Voices carried towards him – discussing, arguing, placating. Beyond them a low moan, like the wind, like a Zom-Boyz crowd during the third number, like the brain-dead crooning for the medicine that kept them functioning, if not entirely alive.

Billy returned with a young fan arm in arm. Roddy

suspected that she was seriously underage. Her jeans were designer chic; her eyes were clear, for now.

"Police Chief's daughter is a big fan," Billy beamed. "Turns out the gig can go ahead. We're going to let little Lottie here ride to the show with us."

"Just don't overwork your hands," Roddy suggested.

"As if," Billy answered.

The crowd was wilder than ever this time around. Reaching, lurching, moaning...

Roddy knew his rock history and worried that tonight would witness another stampede, a fatal surge, a crushing of young bodies. He had reformatted "Love Is the Vein" into a slow, moodily acoustic ballad and there was no reason for anyone to mosh. Yet here they came again, an inhuman wave of devotion, desire and hysteria.

There, one of the barriers was down. The security team repositioned themselves to try to plug the leak; to hold back these grasping young women, teenagers and even pre-pubescent girls who were desperate to get to their idols, to grab a piece of them, be it clothing, flesh, or even soul.

Patterson was signalling frantically from the side of the stage. Roddy realized that Glen had already unplugged his bass and Billy had vacated his padded drum stool. Essentially, Roddy had been crooning to himself, lost in the moment; even as he was aware of the danger posed by the fans he had also entered that rare space in his brain that opened when he was in his most creative, ego-free state. So sad to leave that holy place, the land without thoughts. Just being. Like a non-dead zombie.

And there came the cry, audible from the rioting crowd, "Zom-Boyz! Zom-Boyz!"

Rock 'n' roll to the core, Roddy strummed a final

chord and raised his guitar above his head in omnipotent salute for five seconds before strolling offstage.

As he neared the exit, Patterson – wide-eyed, red-faced – strode into his personal space and cuffed him twice about the head.

"What the fu—"

"Shut the fuck up, moron. You got a death wish? That mob want to tear you limb from limb. They've already accounted for two of the local bouncers. Grab your spangly jacket from the dressing room and run for the bus. The whole situation has gone tits up."

The bus rumbled on, the taciturn driver mostly concealed within a Plexiglas cocoon. Roddy eased his cabin door open a little. The coast seemed to be clear. He lit his way with the illumination from his phone. The device wasn't picking up much of a signal out here on the highway. Tantalising snippets of info about an unfolding catastrophe elsewhere in the country; maybe elsewhere in the world, it was difficult to tell when you couldn't get access to ABC News, Fox News or even the *Huffington Post*. Maybe when they reached the next town there would be a few more masts to aid reception. In the meantime, best not to let Patterson see him up and about with the device. Pad his slightly wobbly way to the chemical toilet and then back to bed.

A click from one of the other doors had him turning around like the surprised hero in a slasher flick.

"Oh, hey, Billy, it's just you. Restless night, huh?"

"It's not me that's restless, Roddy, it's this girl Lisa I picked up at the gig. We've been at it for hours and now she's got the munchies!"

Right on cue, a semi-clad female appeared behind the drummer, moaning incomprehensibly. Her small pointed fingers stretched to brush past Billy, clutching vaguely at his mussed hair, the coach wall, thin air...

"Fuck, Billy!" Roddy offered in a harsh whisper. "You picked up a girl last night. Are you mad?"

"Take it where you can get it, man, is my motto. Although this one has pretty much exhausted me. Haven't you, doll?"

He turned back towards Lisa and began another slobbery kiss, his hand ensuring that her left breast finally popped out of her unbuttoned blouse. She worked at his mouth like she was giving CPR. The need for regular food seemed to have abated for a while. She dragged Billy towards her, her legs beginning a slow grind like an upright spider ensnaring its prey. Billy resurfaced once to catch his breath; muttered, "Laters!" over his shoulder.

Roddy returned to his bed, took out his old acoustic guitar from beneath the bunk, strummed quietly for a while. Was this what rock music was all about? Being a marauding Viking intent on raping, looting and pillaging the land? Were the Zom-Boyz merely a pale, modern imitation of the infamous tours conducted in the distant past by the likes of Led Zeppelin? Girls treated as meat; shows treated as triumphal parades; band members almost untouchable beyond their coterie of muscular guardians?

And yet... was there some sort of complicity on the part of their audience, maybe even a yearning need? Are they milking us dry or am I just excusing my questionable behaviour? he asked himself, putting down the Fender and trying to settle to sleep.

Roddy was holed up in the chemical toilet. His bowels were fine; he had chosen the location as a spot where he could receive intermittent internet and digital coverage. And that's all it was: intermittent. But he had put enough clues together to know that things weren't right across the whole continent; heck, the whole world, even those Taliban type places that didn't let out much news to the watching Western eyes. The plague had spread its unloving tentacles across the globe, bringing an unpredictable, extended death. The higher cognitive functions went pretty early; some of the vocal abilities and motor functions held on for some time afterwards. As long as you didn't become too dumb ass to remember to keep eating and drinking. Pepsi cola, Jack, burgers, blood, brains... whatever your grasping hands could get hold of, in fact.

Sounds like most of those drugs the pushers bring around to the dressing room door when Patterson isn't looking, Roddy smirked.

He tapped a few keys, called up his personal blog. Might as well save a few thoughts even if he couldn't post them.

"For some time we have thought that we are one of the focal points of world culture. Everywhere that we go there are news cameras, MTV, MSN and the like following us, wanting to know what we think about music, fashion, hot girls, whatever. Somewhere along the way in this meandering tour we have slipped out of the nexus; perhaps even been expelled. The world has turned and we have been thrown out of the centre into the margins. Things have progressed *not so nicely* without us. We no longer matter. If we ever did.

"I shall write about it all in song one day. Something a little more reflective and lyric-heavy than our previous output. Something a little more mature. If we survive that far..."

Patterson had halted the bus and ordered everybody off. The female stowaway was summarily given her marching orders. Billy pleaded Lisa's case in the cripplingly hot sunshine. Patterson gave the young woman a bottle of mineral water. Her expressionless eyes took no notice; her hands failed to grip. Clyde stepped over, turned her through one hundred and eighty degrees and with deceptive ease sent her walking on her way.

"Fucking Zom-Girlz!" Patterson moaned.

"I wish I was," Billy muttered.

One of the crew had spread a whole bunch of old-fashioned paper maps and guide books across the side of the dirt road. Word had reached the driver that the next town was impassable and that tomorrow's destination was a city in flames with rioting and violent disorder its current default setting. More pressing was the need to fill up on diesel.

Patterson pointed at a tiny symbol on one of the atlases. "There's a diner and filling station twenty miles east. Reckon we can make it if we keep the speed steady."

Half an hour later found the lot of them parking up at Jim's Fill You Up. Patterson was first off the vehicle, his charm the masses face displaying the worth of all its twenty thousand bucks dentistry.

The proprietor – bizarrely Hank, not Jim – was still accepting dollars and could quickly rustle up several plates full of burgers for hungry rock stars once he'd pumped a hundred gallons or so into the coach's tank. He was playing what Roddy at first took to be a country station. Maybe find out how badly the world teetered... It proved to be an iPhone hook-up: no news and no adverts interrupting his pre-recorded choice of Shania, Dolly and Kenny classics.

"What next?" Roddy asked Patterson as he wiped the last of the ketchup from his young face.

"I shouldn't say this, I should play the stern father figure to the very end, but I'm at a loss, kid. I know you've been checking things on your cell. Maybe this is the very end. At the moment, I'm too full to do anything but maybe have a snooze and see what occurs once the heat's gone out of the day."

Roddy left him to it. Standing at the side of the highway with a wide-brimmed hat protecting his dark hair and sharp eyesight, he could see no vehicles in any direction. No sign of a town, either. Where did Jim/Hank pick us his regular trade or even supplies from? This was truly the middle of nowhere. Headlining the Cow Palace and the Filmore seemed a million years and as many miles away at this point.

After ten minutes or so, he caught movement over to the west. Was this the fabled mirage, more often associated with the Sahara but equally applicable to any arid, superheated landscape?

There were some binoculars in the glove compartment of the bus. Roddy considered retrieving them but decided instead just to hold his ground.

To his surprise, Patterson appeared at his side. "It's a crowd of people," the manager announced after a short, squinting pause. "Looks like our audience is coming to us, kid."

Soon a low keening could be heard. One might have recognized it as words... but primitive, guttural, lusting.

"Get the kit set up!" Patterson ordered. "Tell Clyde or Donaldson to rig up the power through the bus's engine. Come on, start playing... it's our only hope."

What to play to soothe the massing crowd? It had to be an epic, extended version of "Love Me Like a Zombie". How long his fingers could keep flattening the strings in this weather would remain to be seen. For now, just indulge...

Two hours in and the situation seems calm and mostly

under control. There has been much fornicating and other expressions of love and devotion by the massed audience; the outbreaks of crowd-surfing followed by sucking and squelching noises has formed a weird timpani accompaniment to Billy's solid rhythm. But the fans have held off from actually touching their idols for now.

Patterson nods and gives the signal for the boys to leave their equipment still broadcasting on feedback and make a dash for the bus.

It almost works. Donaldson has the engine running but the gears stick and they lose vital seconds. The bus is surrounded by Amazons, blocking off all escape routes.

Glen chooses this moment to break his habitual silence: "They don't just want our bodies they want our brains."

"Well your brains have always been inside your pants, so no fear," Patterson shoots back, Glasgow gallows humour holding till the last. But his eyes betray his true feelings.

Billy is already at the main door, a half-full bottle of Jack Daniel's under his arm. "It's the final countdown!" he announces.

"You can't go out there!" Roddy yells.

"Can and will," Billy answers. The security light makes a halo effect behind his tousled head as he delivers his final sermon. "Guys, I've drunk nearly enough to be as brain dead as that mob out there. I reckon we should enjoy this last night of freedom and free thinking, get absolutely legless and then embrace our inner and outer zombie. Anyhow, some of them girls that I've seen are right hot bitches. I ain't gonna pass them up. Sure. I know they maybe smell a bit but, hey, it all comes down to a bit of meat at the end of the day. There's a cute little redhead with most of her

T-shirt ripped away. Gorgeous tits. Not decomposed at all."

Roddy can stand it no longer: "You're an idiot. You're seriously going to go out there and try to shag them half-dead mothers. You'll catch something fatal even if they don't scoop out your brains first."

Billy grins and already his eyes are not quite normal. "Nah, look at it this way," he drawls, "no need for condoms; fucking *au naturel*. They sure as hell ain't gonna get pregnant. Won't live long enough."

Then he is gone – to the grasping hands, the groaning mouths, the writhing legs.

Roddy reaches for his guitar. Is he going to write a sonic requiem? Is he going to take his guitar with him as an adjunct to every sexual conquest, somewhat in the manner of a modern day Hendrix? Or is he going to use it as a weapon to ward off the loving fans come to reclaim his troubled soul, taking a reckoning of all the callow and thoughtless things he's done?

Billy has left the door open. A wave of sexually crazed humanity ascends the drop stairs.

"Zom-Boyz!" they croon.

Len Saculla has had stories and poems published in venues such as the BFS publication Dark Horizons, Terry Grimwood's Wordland and Ian Hunter's Unspoken Water. He has also had a couple of stories turned into podcasts from Joanna Sterling's "Tube Flash at the Casket" (www.thecasket.com).

"Surprise Thee Ranging With Thy Peers"

The Two Husbands #3

Walt Brunston

"Get back, monster!" yells Husband One. He is in quite a fix. His left eye, left arm and left leg are in the late Cretaceous period, being menaced by a dinosaur, but his right eye, right arm and right leg are apparently in the nineteenth century, warding off one of Napoleon's soldiers in a thicket. He twists his mouth to the right side of his face. "Leave me alone, Frenchy!"

"Anglais!" is the shout, and Husband One regrets having spoken. Not a good time to be an English speaker in France!

"Non, non, Americain! Ami! Ami!"

"Oui, Americain?" The soldier lowers his sword. "I speak a little American."

The dinosaur is not being quite as friendly. It looks to Husband One like a triceratops, though his knowledge of dinosaurs is not extensive. It doesn't seem like it wants to eat him, but it seems very angry with him. He turns to look left and right, closing his right eye to concentrate on the Cretaceous era.

There! He sees the eggs of the triceratops, nestled in a mound mere centimetres away from his feet.

"Ah ha, no wonder you're angry!" he says, screwing his mouth over to the left. He begins to step slowly away from the nest, raising his left arm and nodding his head slowly. "I don't want to hurt anyone. Please just let me leave."

He suspects that the triceratops won't be able to understand him, but it's worth a try.

Unfortunately the Frenchman is not reassured. "Where are you going, my friend?" He lifts his sword up again. "And for that matter, where is the other half of you? Are you some kind of demon? Not that we believe in such things nowadays, of course."

Husband One stops moving, closes his left eye, opens his right eye, screws his mouth over to the right side.

"I'm sorry, monsieur, I mean no disrespect. The reason for my strange half-man appearance is that I have been divided between two times. The half of my body that you can see is in your time, in the year...?"

"1810."

"Thank you. This half is in 1810, while the half of my body that you cannot see is at present trapped in the past, where it is being threatened by a dinosaur, a maman, who worries for her eggs. I do not wish to alarm you by moving suddenly, but I can at present feel that dear lady nudging me in the ribs, her impatience evident. Please, good sir, please allow me to step a few metres further back so that she can be assured I have no plans to feast upon her young."

"Sir," says the Frenchman, "I struggle to understand all of your words, but what I can see of your visage seems trustworthy. Please take all the steps you need to take, and we shall recommence our dialogue once both halves of your person are safe."

"I thank you from the bottom of my heart," says Husband One.

He closes his right eye, opens his left eye, and scrunches his mouth over to the left side of his face.

The triceratops is awfully close. She stares at him with one eye, then twists her head around to look at him with the other. He tries to smile at her, so far as that is possible while keeping one's mouth on one side of one's face.

"I am sorry for troubling you, madam, and now I shall be walking away, very slowly!" He takes first one step away, and then another, and she seems happy about this, to the extent that he feels bold enough to give her a friendly pat on the nose with his left hand. "Good lass!" He takes greater steps back and is soon well away from her precious eggs. He gives her a friendly wave, walks a bit further to find a nice spot under a tree, and takes a seat.

How interesting, he thinks, to have one half of his body sweating in the heat of the late Cretaceous, and the other shivering in the Napoleonic winter. He presumes that given time the two would even out, as blood and heat circulate through his body. Right now it just feels weird.

He opens his right eye, but this time leaves his left eye open. It is like looking through a microscope, he thinks. You get used to it after a while. It helps that he is not walking around or having a dinosaur poke him with her nose! To achieve the same effect for yourself, go to a place in your house where two doors to two rooms stand side by side, and use your hands to create a barrier so that each eye can only see one room. Your brain makes sense of it. It's clever, your brain! And so it is for Husband One. It is strange, naturally, but his life is often very peculiar.

"So tell me, American," says the French soldier, "is there any way in which I can help you out of your unfortunate predicament?"

"What do I look like?" asks Husband One. "From the side, I mean. Can you see right into my guts?"

The French soldier walks around to have a better view. Or a worse view, one would imagine! Who wants to see a stomach gurgling happily away except a gastrointestinal surgeon?

"Non, monsieur," says the Frenchman, who despite his friendly demeanour is beginning to resent the fact that Husband One has not yet troubled to ask the Frenchman's name. "I cannot see a thing. It is as if a morning Lille mist hangs over your side, protecting your insides from my inquisitive eyes."

"Try hitting it with your sword," Husband One says. "No! Wait! Not with the pointed end – just in case!"

The Frenchman nods. "Forgive my foolishness." He whacks the hilt of his sword against Husband One's exposed middle. There is a crack of lightning, a flash of the dark, and the Frenchman is thrown back six feet. But he is not knocked out, and is back at the side of Husband One before the latter has time to even get to his feet.

"What was that? You didn't feel it, monsieur?"

"No, not a thing, not on my left side nor my right. That gap is not me, not part of me. I think you were hitting time itself. I shouldn't have asked you to do that so casually. You could have died."

"Happily I did not."

"All very curious," says Husband One, who has just realised that he has not yet introduced himself, nor asked for the Frenchman's name, but wonders whether the conversation has gone too far to make introductions possible without a great deal of awkwardness. No, it has not. He is not English, after all. "I am known as Husband One," he says, holding out his right hand for a shake. "I am part of a crimefighting partnership by the name of the Two Husbands."

"Les deux maris! Fantastic. Les deux femmes, they approve of your adventuring?"

"Let's just say that we adventure as we choose, whether others approve or not."

"Magnifique! That is truly the way of honour. My own name is Gustave. Gustave de Tourcoing. But your carefree adventuring seems to have landed you in trouble!"

"A rascal by the name of Tortoisio. He had a tortoise in his head, strange as that may sound."

"I am talking to half a man," says Gustave, sitting himself down on a log and pulling some dried meat from his bag. "Nothing could sound stranger."

"He had a weapon, a strange musket of the future, one I think he had made himself. He fired it at me, and I thought I was dead, but here I am, half in your time, half in that of the dinosaurs."

"The dinosaurs, monsieur?"

"Giant creatures that lived on the earth long before mankind."

Gustave chews thoughtfully for a moment before replying. "It would seem, monsieur, that the answer is to bring the two halves of yourself back together. Could you wait here for your other half to catch up?"

Husband One shakes his head, or, from Gustave's point of view, his half a head. "Non. Time is moving at the same speed for both parts of my body, as far as I can tell."

"This gun the madman built, you saw it, can you build one too?"

"No," says Husband One. "The technology is not available here in France, and even less so back in dinosaur times." It is very uncomfortable for him to talk at such length from one side of his mouth. Try it yourself!

Gustave stands at his full height and stretches out his arms. "Monsieur, I believe there has been something of a misunderstanding between us, which wounds me to the very essentials since we have been in such sympathy since resolving the unpleasantness of our initial encounter! We are not in France!"

"We are not?"

"No, monsieur! Just because I am a Frenchman, you think I must live in France? This is the modern age! There are Frenchmen everywhere!"

The thicket fades away, dissolving as if it were just an illusion, and Husband One realises that it was. He is standing in a huge grey crater on the moon, and in the distance he can see puffs of smoke drifting ever so slowly from the open mouths of muskets. He is on the moon, with a Napoleonic soldier. In 1810.

Or at least half of him is.

His day is not getting any better.

"We are on the moon, monsieur! We just like to make it look like home when we are not fighting."

"Husband Two," shouts Husband One at planet Earth, floating like a big blue idiot in the black sky above. "Pull your finger out and rescue me from this lunacy! This is not what I meant when I said I hoped to lose some weight!"

Then he has a think, and shouts the same thing again, really, really, really slowly.

Walt Brunston's adaptation of the classic television story, Space University Trent: Hyperparasite, is now available on Kindle.

The Quarterly Review

Reviews by
Douglas J. Ogurek,
Stephen Theaker
and Jacob Edwards

Douglas J. Ogurek's *work has appeared in the BFS Journal, The Literary Review, Morpheus Tales, Gone Lawn, and several anthologies. He lives in a Chicago suburb with the woman whose husband he is and their pit bull Phlegmpus Bilesnot. Douglas's website can be found at: www.douglasjogurek.weebly.com.*

Jacob Edwards flies with Australia's speculative fiction flagship Andromeda Spaceways Inflight Magazine, but meets us in the pub between runs. This writer, poet and recovering lexiphanicist's website is at www.jacobedwards.id.au. He also has a Facebook page at www.facebook.com/ JacobEdwardsWriter, where he posts poems and the occasional oddity. Like him and follow him!

STEPHEN PALMER *Beautiful Intelligenc*

AI or BI? Artificial intelligence or beautiful intelligence?

The race to create a sentient machine is headed by two teams, led by former researchers at Ichikawa Laboratories, who escape the regime there – and each other – to pursue their own dreams in the world beyond Japan.

Leonora Klee is creating a single android with a quantum computer brain, whose processing power has never before been achieved.

Manfred Klee is creating a group of individuals, none of them self-aware, in the hope that they will raise themselves to consciousness.

But with a Japanese chase team close on their heels, will either be successful before they are trapped and caught?

Beautiful Intelligence is a fast-paced, philosophical thriller that confronts questions of how we will create artificial sentience, and whether it will be *beautiful*.

Stephen Palmer's new SF novel is published 1 July by Infinity Plus Books.
"His work is unique, original, sometimes challenging, always fresh..." (Gary Dalkin)

Audio

Holy Cow

Review by Stephen Theaker

Holy Cow (Macmillan Audio; Audible edition) by David Duchovny. Subtitled a modern-day dairy tale, *Holy Cow* is the story of Elsie, a cow who discovers the grim fate awaiting her kind in the slaughterhouse. With Shalom the pig and Tom the turkey she makes a break for it. Animals can talk to each other through grunts, whistles, barks and squeals, "a kind of universal beastly Esperanto", which will come in handy as they travel the world. Elsie hopes to reach India, where cows are revered. Shalom dreams of Israel, where no one eats pork, and he's already using Yiddish words and phrases and planning his circumcision. Tom is heading for Turkey, but his real dream is to fly.

It's a short book, lasting just three hours, broken up into forty-eight chapters. Duchovny reads the audiobook himself, and is much more laid-back than fans of *Californication* might have expected – it's friendly and conversational, rather than intense and tortured. That's not to say he isn't talking about some big stuff: our treatment of animals, religion, strife in the Middle East. He makes some pretty good points, but the message never overwhelms the charm. I wasn't a fan of the script-like dialogue style, especially early on – it may have looked economical on the printed page, but slows down the audiobook with its repetition – and yet, overall, this is much better than people might have expected.

My favourite character enters the book late on, a camel, a former model, his fame from cigarette advertising appearances now faded, who misses the

adulation that once irritated him so much, and feels guilty about having encouraged people to smoke.
★★★☆☆

More Audio

Stephen Theaker

The Adventure Zone: Murder on the Rockport Limited (Maximum Fun Network) by the McElroys. An excellent podcast where three brothers play *Dungeons & Dragons* with their dad. In this campaign their three daft adventurers are on a non-stop train to Neverwinter, and must pull off a heist and find a murderer before they get there. Their in-character interactions with NPCs like Angus the boy detective

("That's a really good goof, guys!") are what really make it for me. When I was a teenager playing *Warhammer* or *Paranoia* or whatever with my fellow school librarians, I used to laugh so much I couldn't speak. This takes me back to that happy place. ★★★★★

The Brenda and Effie Mysteries: Bat Out of Hull (Bafflegab) by Paul Magrs. Brenda, the former bride of Frankenstein, continues her new life in Whitby, getting tangled up in mysteries with new friend and neighbour Effie. In this second story the entanglement is literal, as Tolstoy, a ventriloquist's felt bat puppet with the uncanny ability to fly on its own, gets stuck in her famous beehive during a performance at the Christmas Hotel. The weirdness with the bat may be connected to the discovery of a toyshop, supposedly established in 1818, though Effie's never heard of it.

The music is perfect, the performances excellent, the story a good one. Never mind Radio 4, this would make perfect Sunday night television. ★★★★☆

Doctor Who: The Beautiful People (Big Finish) by Jonathan Morris. The fourth story from the first series of the Companion Chronicles is an hour-long adventure for the fourth Doctor, K9 and the second Romana, recounted in character by Lalla Ward. The three of them arrive in a beauty spa where the treatments are somewhat extreme. The story ends up offering a positive message towards those of us tipping the scales in the wrong direction, but there's a fair bit of fat description before we get there, and it sounds a bit odd coming from Romana. ★★☆☆☆

Doctor Who: The Blue Tooth (Big Finish) by Nigel Fairs. Third in the Companion Chronicles, from back in 2007. Liz Shaw (played by Caroline John, as on television) recounts an adventure that took place during her brief spell with UNIT. A chum is late for a meeting so Liz pops round to her house: the friend is missing and her cat is dead. There is a befuddled cyberman on the loose, and it'll take Liz and the third Doctor four short episodes to sort it out. ★★★☆☆

Doctor Who: The Catalyst (Big Finish) by Nigel Fairs. Louise Jameson returns to the role of Leela, the fourth Doctor's second female companion. They visit Lord Douglas, who turns out to have travelled with a previous incarnation of the Doctor for several years and now has a secret trophy room full of mementos. His reasons for leaving the Tardis play an important role in the story. After initial frostiness, Leela warms up to Lord Douglas's daughter, Jessica, who likes Rudyard Kipling and speaks with admiring horror of the suffragettes, and they discover that there is yet another secret within the trophy room, a secret with golden hair and wide, glistening eyes... The Doctor has taught Leela not to judge by appearances, but it's a lesson Jessica may not get the chance to learn. This is the fourth story of the second series of the Companion Chronicles, and after listening to several of these in a row it's hard not to feel the contrivance behind the various interviews and interrogations each companion must undergo. We're grown-ups, could we not just agree to accept that Leela is telling us a story without a framing device? It's also odd to hear a companion doing impressions. Sometimes it works well, but, as Louise Jameson acknowledges in an interview postscript to the story, her approximation of Tom Baker doesn't quite work, sounding a bit like William Hague with a sore throat. Her Leela, though, is still fantastic, and the story gives her some full-blooded villains to chew on. ★★★☆☆

Doctor Who: Helicon Prime (Big Finish) by Jake Elliott. Story two in the second series of Companion Chronicles. Frazer Hines plays Jamie McCrimmon, who shouldn't remember anything of his adventures with the second Doctor, but for some reason he does, and he's telling someone all about one of them. While Victoria is off studying graphology, the Doctor and Jamie land by accident on Helicon Prime, a luxury resort, booked up decades in advance and parked in a bit of space that keeps everyone unnaturally nice and peaceful. (It was moved there after visiting couples had shown a tendency, once they had a chance to relax and really think about things, to realise their mutual loathing and murder each other.) But someone must be immune, because there is a mysterious death, and then another, and now the Doctor's got a real job on his hands. This story had some lovely incidental music that combined with the aliens and ambassadors to

remind me quite a bit of *Mass Effect*. We get to hear how Jamie feels when the Doctor keeps him in the dark, and how he decides what to do in those situations. One dialogue exchange is as good as anything from the television series: "What are you thinking?" asks Jamie. "I don't know, Jamie," says the Doctor, "I haven't finished thinking it yet." ★★★★☆

Doctor Who: Mother Russia (Big Finish) by Marc Platt. The first story in season two of the Companion Chronicles. Peter Purves returns to the role of Steven, space pilot companion to the first Doctor. In this adventure the two of them and Dodo land in Russia, just as Napoleon prepares to invade, and a rogue alien complicates affairs. The plot requires Steven to be a bit dopey, but the Russia of 1812 is a fascinating setting

and overall this really does have the feel of an authentic story from the Hartnell period. ★★★★☆

Doctor Who: Old Soldiers (Big Finish) by James Swallow. The third story from series two of the Companion Chronicles is an hour-long adventure with Brigadier Lethbridge-Stewart (played by Nicholas Courtney), who recalls an adventure that took place shortly after his decision to kill the Silurians, and perhaps explains his slightly less warlike approach in later stories. A UNIT base in Kriegeskind castle is plagued by the ghosts of ancient soldiers, who still have the power to kill. The Brigadier calls in the third Doctor, who parachutes into the place to help out. A bit reminiscent of *The Ghosts of N-Space*, but much better. ★★★☆☆

Doctor Who: Solitaire (Big Finish) by John Dorney. India Fisher plays Charley Pollard once again, for a story set during her time as companion to the eighth Doctor. He's been turned into a puppet, and she doesn't remember who he is anyway, or why she came into this toy shop in the first place. The owner, a toymaker, is creepy as heck, and a loud voice keeps shouting "PLAAAAY!" This is the twelfth story from series four of the Companion Chronicles, and is a play for two actors rather than the usual monologue by one (with other actors chipping in with their lines). David Bailie is marvellously ripe as the Celestial Toymaker, still smarting from previous defeats at the Doctor's hands. ★★★☆☆

Elvenquest, Series 3 (BBC Audio) by Anil Gupta and Richard Pinto. An Audible collection of the Radio 4 series. The questers continue to search for the fabled sword of Aznagar, and come pretty close to it a couple of times. Along the way they'll meet a wizard who seems rather a lot like Tony Blair, meet the father of Dean the dwarf, and fight Lord Darkness in single combat to decide the fate of the realms (or at least one of them will, and not necessarily the best equipped for the job). Always very funny. ★★★★☆

The Hitchhiker's Guide to the Galaxy: Primary Phase (BBC Audio) by Douglas Adams. Audible edition collecting the Radio 4 series that started it all. Seems strange that I listened to this for the first time so long after watching the television series, reading the books, watching the the film and listening to the audiobook read by Stephen Fry, but the jokes still made me laugh. It had never clicked before that the extracts from the Guide had originally served as introductions and recaps for each episodes. Very much looking forward to the next three phases. ★★★★★

Books

The Dark Defiles

Review by Jacob Edwards

The blood wells, the ink heralds.

Richard Morgan seemed to spend most of *The Steel Remains*, the first book of his *A Land Fit For Heroes* trilogy, coming to terms with his own dark take on the fantasy genre. The ending was abrupt (almost like walking off a cliff), and it took him much of the second book, *The Cold Commands*, to prod and coerce his protagonists back into the story. These characters, however, were always the key, and having made his name writing holistic and gritty science fiction, Morgan, from the moment he embarked upon his disquieting march across genre boundaries, clearly wasn't going to start faffing about with bog-standard wizards and warriors, chalices and chosen ones; nor, for that matter, join-the-dot quest narratives, rainbow character arcs or pre-industrial paradises threatened by long-dormant evil forces now risen. The setting would be, as the umbrella title suggested, one calling out for heroes, but those heroes in turn would be the tarnished product of their environment. By nature of his approach, Morgan implicitly promised (then explicitly delivered) the sort of unsettling realism that sees shires ransacked and Hobbits crushed dead underfoot. The result is urgent, forceful, unromantic, *unforgettable* – including graphic, present tense flashbacks to defining acts in the protagonists' lives, some of them sexual and uncensored, brazenly confronting – yet, by spurning escapism and the lazy warm glow of the happily ever after, could Morgan, for all his exertions and for all that his titles play coy with noun/verb ambiguity, ever have thought to leave us with fantasy sutras as satisfying as they are compelling? The answer, of course, lies in the trilogy's concluding book, **The Dark Defiles** (Gollancz, 549pp).

Morgan's brand of high fantasy differs from the

WINNER OF THE ARTHUR C. CLARKE AWARD

RICHARD K. MORGAN

THE DARK DEFILES

BOOK THREE OF *A LAND FIT FOR HEROES*

historically popular model in several key aspects, the most pervasive of which is a grimness of setting; the stark refusal to glamorise a world in which the overwhelming majority of the population is poor, miserable, vulnerable and without prospect. *A Land Fit for Heroes* is not, in short, a place that right-minded readers would wish themselves into, not even (or perhaps especially not) as the heroes in question. Morgan's main characters – Ringil, an outcast homosexual swordsman; Archeth, an immortal drug addict orphaned of her alien heritage; and Egar, an aging nomad and onetime dragon-slayer too restless to settle – have their own codes to live by, certainly, but they are more self-serving than altruistic or noble; as much as their particular natures have inured them to the heroism (such that it is) of railing against life's misfortunes and limitations, their dogged struggle for self-determinism rarely appears more than a rearguard action. As *The Dark Defiles* builds towards its conclusion, the plot doesn't so much resolve as clear sufficiently to at last reveal something of Morgan's grand purpose for the trilogy: seemingly, to undermine the tradition, to question the very concept, of an externally mandated quest. Yes, Ringil, Egar and Archeth are on a quest (or, more accurately, three quests with considerable overlap), but the defining difference is that they are not instruments of some greater need; rather, the course of events is shaped by *their* needs. They are not recruited to the quest; they generate its existence. Morgan's crowning accomplishment, then, is to leave his players unaware that they are part of any great undertaking, while slyly inculcating in the reader an appreciation that fantasy is, ultimately and at its best, about the intricacies of *who*, and that *where* and *why*, and *what* and *how* and *when*, are merely tributaries and run-off in an ever-refining, ever-defining cycle of identity.

With *The Steel Remains* having broken new ground as an audacious if incomplete challenge to genre platitudes, and *The Cold Commands* then coming on again as unremitting and unflinching, near enough self-contained, a high-water mark, *The Dark Defiles* remains faithful to Richard Morgan's rose-thorn-scratched not rose-tinted ethos; inaccessible, perhaps, without the preceding books, but cleverly resolved and feeding synergy back into the mix, allowing the trilogy to reach a most apposite, far from inevitable conclusion. If Tolkien laboured over every detail, every where, why, what, how and when of *Lord of the Rings*, Morgan has sweated blood on the who of *A Land Fit for Heroes*. In the perfect world he so emphatically disavows, this would see him take pride of place for the next fifty-plus years. As it is – well, chances are he'll just have to suck it up and keep on doing what he does. But such is the way of heroes.

More Books
Stephen Theaker

The Agonizing Resurrection of Victor Frankenstein (Subterranean Press) by Thomas Ligotti. Short-shorts that put alternative spins on well-known stories. ★★★☆☆

All You Need Is Kill (Haikasoru) by Hiroshi Sakurazaka. An sf take on *Groundhog Day*, it's neat and thrilling without making tons of sense. Filmed as *Edge of Tomorrow*, where Tom Cruise plays a journalist who appears for just a second in the book. Here, it's a soldier who keeps dying and waking up again, and gets better and better at fighting. ★★★☆☆

Black Hat Jack (Subterranean Press) by Joe R. Lansdale. Western adventure. ★★★★☆

The Great Bazaar & Brayan's Gold (Tachyon Publications) by Peter V. Brett. A courier travels through mountains haunted by rock demons, and tries to recover precious pottery from a village abandoned to sand demons. Enjoyable enough. My review appeared in *Interzone* #259. ★★★☆☆

The Life-Changing Magic of Tidying (Ebury Digital) by Marie Kondo. I've mentioned before in TQF that I barely read prose books in print any more, and when I do they are generally review copies. And yet my house is full beyond full with them. Before I bought this terribly helpful book the piles of books on the coffee table in my office were almost a metre high. Kondo offers some excellent advice: hold the item in your hand, and see if it sparks any joy in you. That has made it much easier to triage my collection, and I've been throwing books out by the dozen ever since. I'd like to say the point is almost in sight where I can fit all of my remaining books on our bookcases, but I'm nowhere near. (Anyone who has read Kondo's book will know that means I haven't been following her advice to the letter – she says to do it all in one go.) But it has been nice to see the rubbishy books begin to disappear from my shelves to be replaced by books I truly treasure. There were at least a dozen historical fiction novels in my collection that I had rescued from the discard pile at our school library and carried around with me for a quarter of a century, with no real intention of ever reading them. Now gone! And it did make me sad. But I took photos of them, and if I ever develop the desire to read any of them I'm sure I'll be able to track a new copy down. ★★★★☆

The Merchant and the Alchemist's Gate
(Subterranean Press) by Ted Chiang. An alchemist tells
a merchant a series of stories about the people who
have used his magical gate – one side takes you into
the past, the other into the future. It's a stylish and
clever take on the style of the Arabian Nights.
★★★★☆

Tortured Souls: The Legend of Primordium
(Subterranean Press) by Clive Barker. This collects
short stories that originally appeared in the packaging
of a series of action figures, so it's a bit disjointed, but
I liked the idea that on Sunday God, rather than
resting, made all the monsters. ★★★☆☆

**Welcome to Just a Minute! A Celebration of
Britain's Best-Loved Radio Comedy** (Canongate
Books) by Nicholas Parsons. Read in a single day!
Fascinating anecdotes of tetchiness, bitchiness and no
little affection among the *Just a Minute* regulars.
Almost enough to make me forgive Parsons for the
time we took the children to his supposedly PG-rated
Edinburgh show. You can't trust anyone these days!
★★★★☆

The Whispering Swarm (Tor Books) by Michael
Moorcock. A character called Michael Moorcock
becomes a professional writer, while cheating on his
wife and making regular visits to an abbey connected
to all time and space by way of the moonbeam road.
It's a fascinating book, but as a novel it slumps badly
in the middle before ending well. Maybe they should
have sold it as an autobiography and let the fantasy
elements come as a surprise. Reviewed for *Interzone*
#258. ★★★☆☆

The Young Dictator (Pillar International Publishing) by Rhys Hughes. Jenny Khan is a young English girl who decides to stand for MP of her town, and with the help of her nefarious gran rises to become dictator of Britain, then the galaxy, and even hell itself. It's a book packed with the usual Rhys Hughes goofiness, invention and humour. To pick one non-spoilery example, the glossary at the end explains that the astronauts who landed on the moon discovered it has no atmosphere, "because they forgot to take beer and cakes and music". Fun for all ages. The ebook lets the novel down a bit, though: there is a line space between each paragraph, the chapters aren't set up properly, and there's a stingy limit on the number of devices you can read it on. ★★★☆☆

Insightful; scathing; eloquent; witty: like playing charades with a late-night entrenchment of university professors, all in danger of losing their faculties.

Derelict Space Sheep presents

Lemon Moon Review
Sisyphean Night Off

by Jacob Edwards

Spifflication in 25 Film Critiques

Available from www.derelictspacesheep.com

or request a copy through your local library

AU$9.95 paperback   AU$4.95 e-book

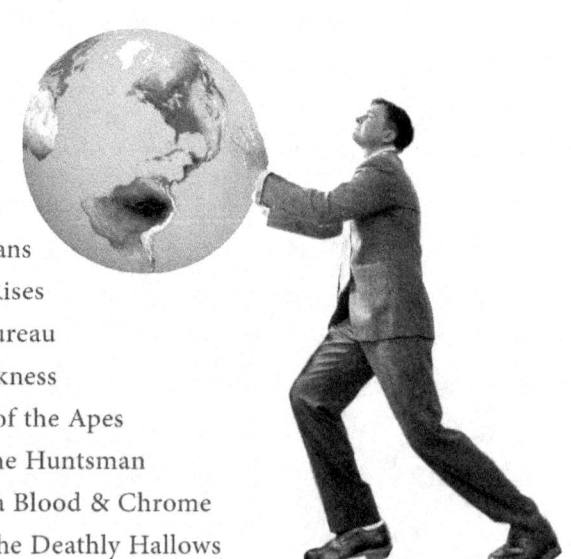

Cathartic; uproarious; irreverent; erudite: beware, any filmmaker who spends less time and effort making a movie than Jacob does in reviewing it.

Comics

The Glorkian Warrior Eats Adventure Pie

Review by Stephen Theaker

The Glorkian Warrior is a Groo-ish idiot whose best friend is his Rufferto-ish Super Backpack, which can shoot lasers and talk, not that the Glorkian Warrior ever takes its advice. The two of them of them previously appeared in a fun iOS game *The Trials of Glork* (reviewed in TQF49) and a graphic novel, *The Glorkian Warrior Delivers a Pizza* (see TQF47).

In that book the Warrior took up the quest to deliver a pizza, as requested by someone who had apparently dialled the wrong number – along the way he became friends with Gonk and a brain-sucking baby alien. The second graphic novel in the series, **The Glorkian Warrior Eats Adventure Pie** (First: Second, hb, 128pp) is as funny and inventive as the first.

In this book they meet Buster Glark, a hiccup-happy jerk with his own super backpack who interferes with their mission: to kill a space snake that destroys fruit pie factories. Later the Glorkian Warrior decides to let his elbow do the thinking while they rearrange the furniture, Gonk comes on Glork Patrol with the phone tied on as his backpack, and the baby alien goes too far in his brain-sucking.

The book is written, drawn, lettered and coloured by James Kochalka, whose glee and silliness is a perfect fit for children's books. I'm not generally one for literary exegesis, but this feels like it grew out of a day he spent goofing around with his own children ("Happy family", "No share no fair!"), and reading it makes you feel like part of the fun.

It's bright and attractive enough to appeal to younger kids, with big clear speech balloons where the words are given plenty of space, and it's eminently re-readable – which I know because I read it again and laughed again while writing this review. Trumping plays a big role, and jokes about that never get old. A joyful read for adults and a perfect book for children, even the most reluctant of readers. Every school should have a copy. ★★★★☆

More Comics

Stephen Theaker

Alien Legion Omnibus, Vol. 2 (Dark Horse Comics) by Alan Zelenetz, Larry Stroman, Frank Cirocco and chums. An okay book of science fiction war stories, with an admirable tendency to kill off its cast and explore the effect that has on the others, but... high heels on the new female recruit's battle armour? What were they thinking? And some of the poses she appears in are ludicrous. ★★★☆☆

The Chimpanzee Complex: Paradox (Cinebook) by Richard Marazano and Jean-Michel Ponzio. An astronaut looking forward to reassignment, and spending more time with her daughter, is required back in space after the astronauts from Apollo 11 splash down – again. The year is 2035. The story is intriguing, reminding me of the first Quatermass Experiment. The art is a bit unusual, looking to me a bit like it's been drawn over photographs, but I got to like it. ★★★☆☆

The Dirty Dozen: The Best 12 Commando Books Ever! (Carlton Publishing Group), edited by George Low. Took me a long time to finish this one. For our overseas readers who haven't heard of *Commando*, it's a small squarish comic of about sixty pages, with a couple of panels per page, telling lots of stories about World War Two, very much in the style of British war films. The stories in this collection are a mixed bag, some tedious, some thrilling. The highlight for me was "Battle-Wagon", about the rivalry between two teams of supply truck drivers racing for the same destination. ★★★☆☆

Empowered, Vol. 5 (Dark Horse Comics) by Adam Warren. Bondage-prone superhero Emp learns more about mysterious Mind—, who stays up in the D10 orbital station to avoid living with everyone's thoughts. Still a very saucy comic, and of course that's much of the appeal, but the superhero stuff gets better and better. ★★★★☆

Empowered, Vol. 6 (Dark Horse Comics) by Adam Warren. Emp grows into her role as a superhero, getting used to her new clinging abilities and even showing some leadership potential after she learns the secret of what happens to dead heroes and their powers. Villain Deathmonger is gathering and enslaving their remnants. Very funny, except when it means to be serious, and it keeps improving. The caged Demonwolf who sits on Emp's coffee table is my favourite tamed baddie since Baytor ("I am Baytor!") in *The Demon*. ★★★★☆

Empowered, Vol. 7 (Dark Horse Comics) by Adam Warren. Ninjette has to deal with a team of bounty-hunting ninjas who want to take her back to the clan she fled with good reason. The book skips about in time to show us the fight, and her training with Emp, and a bathtub conversation with the caged Demonwolf, who for once stops talking like an angry Stan Lee to tell her how he really feels. There is also karaoke. The ongoing storylines progress at a snail's pace, but it's still a great book. The friendship between Emp and Ninjette is as sincere and meaningful as any I've seen in superhero comics. ★★★★☆

JLA, Vol. 5 (DC Comics) by Mark Waidand Bryan Hitch. A disappointment. I love the JLA, and Mark Waid has written some terrific comics, but this just doesn't work. The stories lack decent villains, and the heroes have lost all the sharpness of the Grant Morrison run. I don't know what went wrong here. ★★☆☆☆

Nexus Omnibus 4 (Dark Horse Comics) by Mike Baron, Steve Rude and chums. Much more fun than previous volumes. Nexus himself is far less tortured and conflicted, and heads back to the bowl-shaped world to find a god who might be able to prevent the collapse of Gravity Well, an unstable power station built on a black hole that could destroy the solar system. A band of youngsters from Ylum become huge rock stars, jockeying begins for the presidential elections, and the three girls who pledged vengeance after Nexus executed their father continue their search for enough power to kill him. The backup stories are now all about Judah the Hammer, a huge improvement. The artwork and design is as ambitious and colourful as the stories. My favourite Nexus book yet. ★★★★☆

Nexus Omnibus 5 (Dark Horse Comics) by Mike
Baron and chums. Horatio Hellpop has had enough of
being Nexus, and leaves Ylum to find himself. So the
insane alien Merk grants his power to other
candidates, including three vengeful sisters and a
musclebound professor. Les Dorscheid's colouring

maintains a consistent look despite a succession of guest artists, but with Steve Rude largely absent this book isn't as stylish or distinctive as earlier collections. ★★★★☆

Nexus Omnibus 6 (Dark Horse Comics) by Mike Baron, Hugh Haynes and chums. Alien taskmaster the Merk made Stanislaus Korivitsky the new Nexus, but it's a poor choice: he likes the killing way too much, and when the Merk's power runs out Stan will team up with the Bad Brains! Original Nexus Horatio Hellpop will have to come out of his retirement to take him down. The art on this one has some very shaky moments, but once Hugh Haynes becomes the regular penciller it settles down a bit. Reading these six omnibuses has been a terrific experience, watching Ylum develop into a full-blown society, inching its way forward, making mistakes, trying to balance the varied demands of a growing population. A great science fiction adventure. ★★★★☆

Orbital, Vol. 1: Scars (Cinebook) by Sylvain Runberg and Serge Pellé. A pair of novice special space agents are despatched to Senestam, a moon of Upsall, to resolve the conflict between human colonists and the aliens of Upsall, who would quite like their moon back now that valuable minerals have been found there. Excellent art, and an interesting story, but it is bafflingly split across two slim volumes and the matte printing is unattractive. ★★★☆☆

Orbital, Vol. 2: Ruptures (Cinebook) by Sylvain Runbergand Serge Pellé. The story concludes. £7.99 seems like quite a lot for a 56pp comic. ★★★☆☆

Queen and Country: The Definitive Edition, Vol. 2 (Oni Press) by Greg Rucka, Jason Alexander and Carla

Speed McNeil. Collects three excellent stories about spy Tara Chace and her fellow Minders in the SIS. Like the MI:6 equivalent of *Spooks*. ★★★★★

Star Wars Tales, Vol. 6 (Dark Horse Comics) by Jeremy Barlow. Last and weakest of the series. Too glum, too serious, and too little of the major characters, so that it could try to stay in continuity more. A lot less fun than any of the previous books. ★★★☆☆

Star Wars: Crimson Empire III: Empire Lost (Dark Horse Comics) by Mike Richardson, Randy Stradley, Paul Gulacy, Michael Bartolo and Dave Dorman. The third adventure of Kir Kanos, former guard to Emperor Palpatine, is the first to include Luke, Leia and Han (who seem rather tetchy), but it's the usual story of imperial remnants fighting the new republic and each other. Often hard to tell what's happening in action scenes. ★★★☆☆

Star Wars: Legacy, Vol. 5: The Hidden Temple (Dark Horse Comics) by John Ostrander, Jan Duursema and Dan Parsons. The story steps up a gear, but Cade is still an unpleasant protagonist with terrible hair and Darth Krayt seems more like a He-Man villain than something from Star Wars. I'll keep reading, but only because I bought the whole series in one go. ★★★☆☆

Star Wars: Legacy, Vol. 7: Storms (Dark Horse Comics) by John Ostrander, Omar Fancia, Jan Duursema, Dan Parsons and Brad Anderson. More adventures in the post-Luke future of Star Wars. An imperial knight helps the Mon Calamari fight back against the Sith, underwater, and Cade Skywalker continues his aimless, charmless meanderings around the galaxy. ★★★☆☆

Star Wars: Legacy, Vol. 8: Tatooine (Dark Horse Comics) by John Ostrander, Jan Duursema, Dan Parsons and Brad Anderson. The most obnoxious brat in comics turns to ripping off pirates but they get wise to his force tricks and his stay on Tatooine ends up being longer than planned. Elsewhere in the galaxy far, far away we see how a Mandalorian (like Boba Fett) came to join Rogue Squadron, and what happens when his vengeful ex-wife finds him there. ★★★☆☆

Star Wars: Legacy, Vol. 10: Extremes (Dark Horse Comics) by John Ostrander, Jan Duursema, Brad Anderson and Sean Cooke. Takes the series up to its cancellation with issue 50, though volume 11 continues the story by collecting a mini-series. All the plotlines that have been running keep on running. Cade Skywalker continues to draw on the power of the dark side to fight his enemies and help his friends, while the Sith, former emperors and the remnants of the alliance jockey for galactic power. Readable without being all that exciting. ★★★☆☆

Star Wars: Legacy, Vol. 11: War (Dark Horse Comics) by John Ostrander, Jan Duursema and Dan Parsons. Burdened with much recapping in its early pages, the miniseries collected in this volume still does a surprisingly good job of roosting all the pigeons that flapped around in books one to ten. Cade Skywalker confronts the dark side of the force, the new alliance goes for broke, and the Sith reveal their terrible new weapon. I never grew to love this series, but I read one volume after another, and that tells its own story. It's essentially a thousand-page Star Wars graphic novel. How could I not enjoy it, at least a bit? ★★★☆☆

Star Wars: Vector, Vol. 2 (Dark Horse Comics) by Rob Williams, John Ostrander, Dustin Weaver, Jan Duursema and Dan Parsons. The second half of a crossover between four ongoing Star Wars titles. This contains one story with Luke Skywalker set during the rebellion, and one set over a century later with Cade Skywalker. The connection is a long-lived former Jedi, Celeste Morne, who is bonded with the Muur talisman and the Sith consciousness within it. As well as volume two of *Vector*, this also stands as volume four of *Rebellion* and volume six of *Legacy*, a bizarre set-up that left me searching fruitlessly for the latter after having bought the other ten volumes in a sale. In this book Cade teams up with a trio of Imperial Knights and Celeste Morne to make an assassination attempt on Darth Krayt. It's okay. ★★★☆☆

Thorgal: The Guardian of the Keys (Cinebook) by Grzegorz Rosinski and Jean Van Hamme. Volsung of Nichor steals Thorgal's identity and takes his place among the Vikings. Invincible, thanks to a belt cruelly stolen from the guardian of the keys (it's the only bit of clothing she has!), he begins to murder his way to the kingship. ★★★☆☆

Trekker Omnibus (Dark Horse Books) by Ron Randalland Jim Gibbons. Decent series about a bounty hunter in very tight trousers. A mix of colour and black-and-white stories. ★★★☆☆

Usagi Yojimbo Saga, Vol. 1 (Dark Horse Books) by Stan Sakai. The adventures of a ronin – a masterless samurai – with a conscience. So brilliant even the appearance of the Teenage Mutant Ninja Turtles couldn't harm it. Poetry in every panel. ★★★★★

Films

The Lazarus Effect
Review by Douglas J. Ogurek

Scientist dies, comes back to life, goes on killing spree. What's not to like?

Ever since Dr Frankenstein stitched together his monster, people have been fascinated with laboratory experiments on humans... especially when it comes to what could go wrong.

The Lazarus Effect, Hollywood's latest foray into terror via test tube, explores the repercussions of chemical-based human resurrection. Director David Gelb mixes horror, thriller, and sci-fi elements in a film that, though not staggeringly original, holds up as an elixir for the horror devotee.

Zoe (Olivia Wilde), her too-busy-to-marry beau Frank (Mark Duplass) and science geeks Clay and Niko (Evan Peters and Donald Glover) have spent four years tucked away in a university lab. Their research started with a way to temporarily prolong life, but then evolved – maybe devolved is a better word – into the "Lazarus Serum".

The group first resurrects a dog, but this lab dog is no lap dog. Rocky's erratic behavior and supercharged brain indicate the Lazarus Serum might be more than what it's stirred up to be.

A third of the way through the film, a corporation manoeuvers a hostile takeover of the research and the lab. The infuriated quartet and videographer Eva sneak into the lab to solidify their claim on first to raise the dead. However, when Zoe flips the power switch, she gets electrocuted and dies. Frank convinces his

colleagues to inject the Lazarus Serum into her brain.
Not a well-reasoned decision.

Zoe isn't quite Zoe anymore. The serum has kicked
her brain into hyperdrive. As her nightmares of a girl
in a burning corridor grow more vivid, Zoe develops a
collection of powers straight from the Stephen King
compendium: pyrokinesis, telepathy, telekinesis, and
precognition, to name a few. Of course all these
psychic gifts come with a loss of sanity. Zoe struggles

with whether the colleagues she's locked in the lab want to help her or put her down.

Wilde and Duplass head up a cast of characters whose moderate personalities seem consistent with what one would find in a lab. This lack of eccentricity means more focus on the action. The most energetic scientist is Clay, played by Evan Peters of *American Horror Story* fame. Peters offers a performance reminiscent of (but by no means as outrageous as) a young Philip Seymour Hoffman's Dusty Davis in *Twister*.

Another notable strength of this film is its soundtrack. It starts with the *American Horror Story*-like opening credits: creepy music accompanies extreme close-ups of threatening-looking elements slithering and coalescing. On several occasions, the viewer is treated to Mozart's "The Queen of the Night Aria", which would make watching cell cultures incubate entertaining. During the most intense scenes, a jarring shriek escalates the action in an admirably unsubtle way.

There are masterful lab horror films like *The Fly* and the less well-known *Splice*, and there are their deliciously preposterous cousins like *I, Frankenstein*. *The Lazarus Effect* falls somewhere in the middle. Though the trailer tries to connect it (by way of producer) to *Insidious*, *The Purge*, and *Paranormal Activity*, *The Lazarus Effect* is, by comparison, playing in the minor leagues. Still, many love to (and even prefer to) watch those minor leaguers.

The critics blasted *The Lazarus Effect* with typical complaints: highly derivative, chaotic, an over-qualified cast wasted by an impatient plot. Even the general public has met it with a tepid response.

Nevertheless, there are a few perhaps juvenile viewers who applaud this film, and I, fortunately, count myself among them. ★★★★☆

It Follows

Review by Douglas J. Ogurek

Controlled study in terror rebels against contemporary horror tropes, explores teenage sexuality and parental influence.

The image of *Halloween*'s Michael Myers (1978), with his impenetrable motives, and his patient pursuit of his single-minded purpose (to kill), has embedded itself in the horror aficionado's consciousness. There is something quite unsettling about an impending threat that can't be reasoned with. Clearly John Carpenter's iconic film has influenced writer/director David Robert Mitchell's **It Follows**, which exploits this strategy of approaching doom, coupled with creepy audio and smart filming techniques, to deliver an atmospheric masterpiece in which everything, from the proliferation of soda cans to the pronounced lapping of waves, is rich in implication.

Jay Height (Maika Monroe) is a somewhat woolly-headed teen who likes to lounge in her pool and gaze up at the sky. After she consummates a budding relationship with Hugh, her life takes a turn for the much worse: Hugh passes on a sexually transmitted ghost – can we call that an STG? – that assumes a human form. The ghost pursues the latest person to contract the curse with a Michael Myersesque determination. "It could look like someone you know," says Hugh, "or it could be a stranger in a crowd. Whatever helps it get close to you."

The infected person can divert "It" by sleeping with someone else. However, once it kills the newly infected person, the force moves to the previous person in the chain. Thus Jay is fraught with challenges regarding not only how to evade the pursuer, but also whether and to whom she should pass on the curse.

Neighbourhood heartthrob Greg Hannigan? Awkward long-time family friend Paul? Total strangers?

The Fears of Height
It Follows evades the gore, pop-out scares, and petty squabbles of the typical horror film that has a teenage cast. Its believably lethargic teens engage in mundane activities (e.g. sitting on a swing, watching an old sci-fi

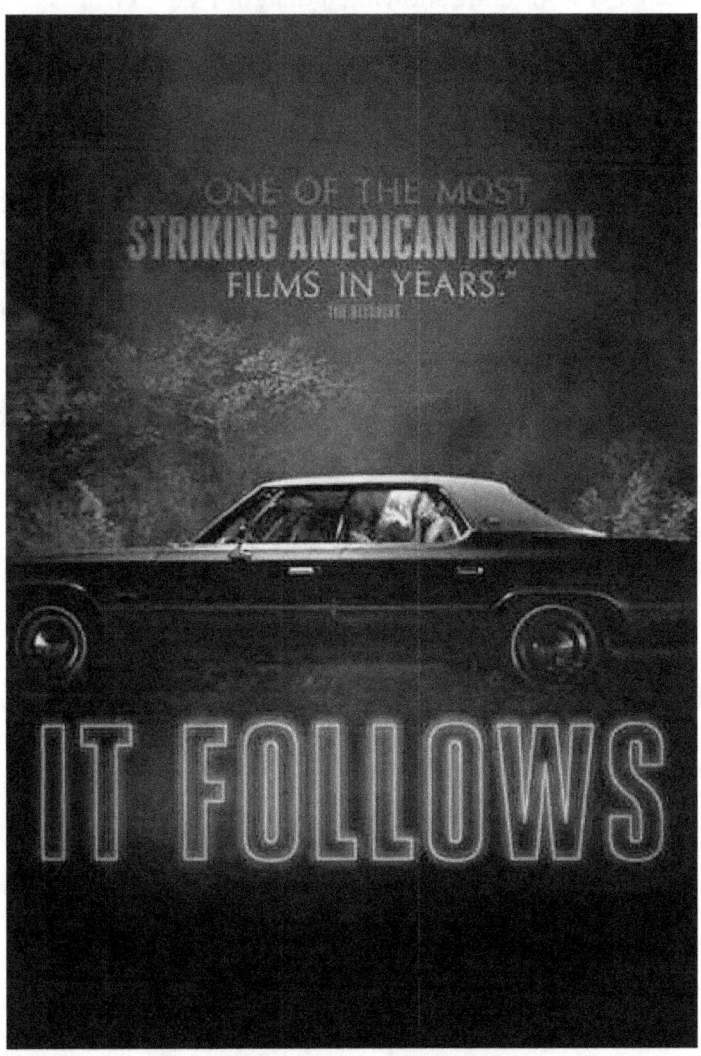

film, lounging on a beach, playing old maid), yet through all of these ostensibly benign scenes lurks the threat.

In one early scene, Jay's professor reads an extended passage from T.S. Eliot's "The Love Song of J. Alfred Prufrock" – the film uses several direct literary quotes – while the camera does a 360 degree pan. It starts with a view outside showing a distant figure (who doesn't quite fit with the other students) walking unsteadily toward the classroom. The camera then slowly pans around the classroom, giving the viewer time to question what he or she saw outside, before the view returns to the courtyard to reveal the figure has come closer.

This isn't the only time Mitchell uses the 360 degree pan. The technique sucks Jay Height and the filmgoer down the drain of this nightmare, and creates a boxed-in feeling: no matter which way you turn, you can't escape this ghost.

The use of sound also distinguishes *It Follows*. This includes the eighties-style synthesizer-heavy tunes of Disasterpeace's soundtrack and the unnerving repetition of sounds (e.g. swing set creaking, waves lapping) amongst otherwise quiet settings.

Additionally, though filmed in Detroit, *It Follows* really takes place in an unknown place, at a time that's hard to pin down. What are we to make of the odd clothing, the dated automobile, and the old television sets despite the present day feel of the film? Why does Jay's friend Yara, with her seventies-style glasses, read Dostoyevsky's *The Idiot* on a shell-shaped e-reader?

Surfaces and Layers
Mitchell seems obsessed with liquids in this film. Jay and company are often near water sources and/or drinking from aluminium cans. Perhaps this is Mitchell's way of challenging us to look below the

surface. Yes, *It Follows* is about a supernatural predator, but it also explores sexual-related repercussions, whether they be STDs or emotional turmoil. In other words, it follows.

Adult figures are conspicuously absent in this film, which challenges the viewer to consider how parents' presence (or lack thereof) in their teens' lives impacts teenage sexual decisions.

The film evokes other questions, the answers to which are beyond the scope of this review. For instance, why is the human form that the ghost adopts often fully or partially exposed? Also, why does the ghost sometimes choose a guise that resembles characters' parents?

What Mitchell has achieved with *It Follows* is a sense of dread that lingers from the strange opening sequence that reveals what "It" is capable of, to the equally disturbing conclusion. See this film, but expect it to follow you long after you've left the cinema.

★★★★★

Avengers: Age of Ultron

Review by Douglas J. Ogurek

Sequel soars with Super Bowl style entertainment.

Our beloved heroes are back to decimate evil, attack our pocketbooks, decrease our IQ, and lavish us with non-stop action.

Avengers: Age of Ultron pumps up the adrenaline of the box office record-breaking *Avengers Assemble* (2012). The sequel stands as a treatise on the values of friendship and loyalty, as well as a commentary on the redemptive qualities of humanity. Plus it has lots of explosions.

Tony Stark (i.e. Iron Man) has a plan to bring peace to Earth through an artificial intelligence called Ultron. However, Ultron's motives (and his take on humans) are a tad less charitable: he wants to destroy humanity. So Ultron makes himself a robotic body, enlists a couple of genetically modified twins ("He's fast, she's weird."), and multiplies his army like "a Catholic rabbit" (Nick Fury's words).

Despite all the biotechnological gobbledygook that passes between Stark and Dr Bruce Banner (the Hulk), the crew has a simple goal: stop Ultron. No matter our willingness to admit it, the reason we adults go to see these films is the same as that of the little boy: to see good guys trounce bad guys. And that's what we get.

Though it's penned by return director Joss Whedon, *Avengers: Age of Ultron* seems to have come together via a think tank of top advertising creatives intent on achieving a two-plus hour Super Bowl commercial. From the opening snowy battle scene to the rollicking conclusion, the film keeps the viewer hypnotised with its rock star cast and cartoonish fight sequences.

In this film, plot is peripheral to action. It's best viewed on a big screen. A robot-propelled semitrailer floating above New York just isn't the same on a small screen.

According to the National Center for Biotechnology Information, the attention span of the average American dropped 33% between 2000 and 2013. We're at about eight seconds. The makers of *Avengers: Age of Ultron* got the memo.

Something for Everyone

The film appeals to many different ages and cinematic tastes.

Those who like humour are in for a treat. It's hard to watch the film for longer than two minutes without finding something to at least chuckle at. It starts when Captain America reprimands Stark after he utters the film's first word: "Shit." Soon "Cap" lets slip a dirty word of his own. This becomes an ongoing joke.

The sense of boyish one-upmanship that permeates the film is best encapsulated at a party near the beginning. Thor and Iron Man strive to outbrag each other regarding the accomplishments of their women, Jane Foster and Pepper Potts. The heroes then engage in a strength contest by attempting to lift Mjölnir, Thor's magical hammer. To top it off, Thor enhances the libations with some kind of magical elixir.

For romantics, there's the blossoming relationship between Natasha Romanoff (i.e. Black Widow) and Bruce Banner. It's particularly enjoyable to watch Mark Ruffalo's reluctant, nearly submissive Banner squirm as Scarlett Johansson's character makes clear her interest in him. Sure, Banner is concerned that his green alter ego could tear apart Romanoff, but he's also contending with a much more incredible possibility: that this vixen is actually interested in him despite his supreme nerdiness. Well played by Ruffalo.

For the youngster, especially the hysterical boy who likes to knock things down, *Avengers: Age of Ultron* is a dream come true. Colourful costumes. Robots. Weapons. Razed buildings. Standouts include Captain America's completely unnecessary though enthralling flips and Stark in a souped-up Iron Man getup attempting to stop a mentally altered Hulk's – was it possible for him to get any angrier? – urban rampage.

The film achieves the ultimate in bombastic heroism when the Avengers, positioned in a circle, fight their adversaries as the camera moves around them in slow motion. Absurd. Juvenile. Love it!

Ultron – a Narcissistic Robot with Spunk

The villain that graces millions of bags of chips and cans of soda had better be as bad and as tantalising as the products he touts. Ultron has the crunch and the fizz.

This bad guy combines the appearance of a more agile Terminator robot, the vocal distinctiveness of Heath Ledger's Joker (*The Dark Knight*), and the tangential gems of Christian Bale's Patrick Bateman (*American Psycho*).

James Spader's voiceover shifts from philosophical ennui, to wisecracking commentaries on human frailties (e.g. "Everyone creates the thing they dread... People create... smaller people? Uhh... children! Lost the word there."), to enraged disbelief at others questioning his superiority.

Get ready for a super-sized portion of crackling quotes from this one. After Steve Rogers/Captain America's declaration that there is a way to achieve peace, Ultron says, "I can't actually throw up in my mouth, but if I could I would do it!"

Tony Stark has met his match. ★★★★★

Insurgent

Review by Douglas J. Ogurek

Heroine keeps fighting the system in slightly soppy, though ultimately triumphant sequel.

In *Divergent* (2014), Beatrice "Tris" Prior and love interest Four put a dent in the Erudite/Dauntless alliance (between those who value knowledge above all else, and those who value bravery above all else) aimed at seizing control of a future Chicago whose inhabitants are divided into factions.

This time, **Insurgent**, directed by Robert Schwentke, has the duo on the run from the mental giants at Erudite and the Dauntless goons that they employ.

Tris, distraught by major losses, does what rebellious teenage girls have been doing for years: she chops off her long hair. Perhaps this is a way to shed her grief or redefine herself (or distinguish herself from rival dystopian blockbuster heroine Katniss Everdeen). Then the girl with a boy's hairdo undergoes a series of trials that will shed more light on what she and her Divergent label mean to the future of this world.

Tris and Four undertake a journey that allows the viewer to experience the different factions: the glass dome, green roofs, and farms of the hippie-like Amity; the austere concrete headquarters of the always

truthful Candor; and the gleaming white tower in which the Erudite scheme. *Insurgent* also introduces the lair of the punk rockeresque Factionless, those who are not compatible with any faction and who seek to destroy the existing system to establish a new society.

The film's makers took a great deal of liberty in

manipulating the novel (by Chicagoan Veronica Roth) that inspired it. Characters and major scenes are cut, goals and obstacles are simplified, and key concepts are reimagined. Sure... purists will gripe at such slicing and dicing. However, this film is an entertaining sequel that at its worst resembles a soap opera, but at its best stuns the viewer with breathtakingly technologically indulgent action sequences.

It even treats the viewer to a couple of highly entertaining minor characters. There's the hulking, zero-conscience Dauntless army leader Eric, who looks prepped for an Ultimate Fighting Championship match. Then there's the self-serving smart aleck Peter, played by Miles Teller, star of the Oscar-nominated *Whiplash* (2014). Both Eric and Peter have a knack for pushing Tris's buttons, and push they do.

The standouts in *Insurgent* are Tris (Shailene Woodley) and Erudite mastermind Jeanine Matthews (Kate Winslet).

As in *Divergent*, Woodley proves her ability to convey emotion. Look to the trial scene at Candor headquarters, where Tris is injected with a truth serum. Feel the pain as she struggles to hold back a secret that wracks her with guilt and that will hurt one of the onlookers.

Equally engaging is Winslet's Jeanine Matthews. Veronica Roth's villain isn't very fleshed out: Matthews has no redeeming qualities and no backstory. Considering that Winslet doesn't have a lot to work with, she does a fine job portraying a character that, in a less capable actor's hands, might have been staid (e.g. the antagonist in *The Host* (2013)) or even overblown.

Everything about Matthews is severe: her pulled back hairstyle, her tight blue dress, her economy of movement, her affectless expressions. Whereas Tris is the girl-boy, Matthews is determinedly adult, an undiluted dark monarch who threatens to annihilate those who would bring change to the rigid systems that have been imposed on this society.

In one of the film's most blatant departures from the novel, the filmmakers put the mystery on which this story hangs front and centre in the form of a metallic capsule. Each side of the pentagon contains a faction logo. It sits in a closely monitored room in the Erudite headquarters. Nobody knows what's in the capsule, but it has to be important!

Matthews rounds up those with the highest levels of divergence because the capsule can only be opened when a Divergent passes simulation tests for all five factions. When a test is passed, the corresponding symbol on the capsule illuminates (it must be Wi-Fi compatible). Subjects are attached to snake-like wires that descend from the ceiling, inject substances, and then suspend them in a kind of zero-gravity acid trip. The problem is that a failed simulation means death for the subject.

This capsule is a major simplification of what happens in the book, but it works. Similar to the Tesseract in *Avengers Assemble*, it's as if the filmmakers are saying to characters and the audience, "Here you go... this is what the protagonist needs to open."

There is a term in food industry jargon called "bliss point". It has to do with the amount of unhealthy ingredients (i.e. salt, sugar, fat) needed to maximise taste. During Tris's Dauntless simulation, *Insurgent* achieves a kind of cinematic bliss point. In this technology- and drug-induced sequence, Tris attempts to save a departed loved one in a burning, crumbling house that floats over a city. The scene contains many elements (e.g. dream, intense special effects, damsel in distress) that would make most critics scoff, but to those of us willing to let go, this unapologetic immersion into Hollywood extravagance makes the film worth seeing in the cinema. Legolas would be proud!

The scene also makes up for *Insurgent's* shortcomings, namely too many lovey-dovey scenes, too much dull table talk, and the lackluster personality of Four. When it comes to love, perhaps Tris is a little more certain of her soul mate than Katniss Everdeen or Bella Swan. Great in real life. Boring in film and fiction.

"Defy reality." Such is the challenge that *Insurgent* advertisements pose to the filmgoer. The film, with its simulations, strong polarization between good and evil, and contrasting factions, lives up to its promise and keeps the fictional dream alive. ★★★★☆

Memory Lane

Review by Jacob Edwards

Just when is it safe to go back in the water?

Returning to his home town, troubled young Afghan war veteran Nick Boxer (Michael Guy Allen) finds solace in the love of the inscrutable Kayla M (Meg Braden), a girl with whom he feels an immediate, palpable connection. When Kayla commits suicide, Nick tries to do the same by electrocuting himself, but in the seconds between dying and being revived finds himself re-experiencing moments of their relationship and picking up details he missed when he was alive. Convinced there is more to Kayla's death than first appears, Nick, with the help of close friends Elliot (Julian Curi) and Ben (Zac Snyder), sets out to kill himself again, zapping his consciousness down memory lane as he tries first to understand, then to alter, the past.

Memory Lane (dir. Shawn Holmes) has been likened to Christopher Nolan's *Memento*, an apt comparison insofar as each employs a non-linear plot to explore themes of narrative veracity, grief, memory and perception. Both films were made on relatively low budgets, both are cleverly scripted and both display artfulness not for the cheap thrill of deception but rather for the sake of good story-telling. Yet, whereas *Memento* remains perfectly executed right to the end, *Memory Lane* stumbles at the final hurdle and so must forfeit its standing ovation and receive

only with some caveats the garland of critical acclaim. The subtleties of the story are rendered with a deft touch – particularly the overlap between Nick's mental state post-war and his retroactive acuity while dead – but the denouement feels rushed, and while everything makes sense (air quotes) the reveal does not inspire the audience to an epiphanic fathoming so much as a slow-nodding, piecing-it-all-together sort of reconcilement after the fact.

Memory Lane in this respect bears some resemblance to Shane Carruth's *Primer*, which made a beguilingly naturalistic foray into time travel paradoxes only to fall on the sword of expository narrative voiceover some fifteen minutes short of feature film length. Both movies evidence the best aspects of independent filmmaking: a clear focus on story over spectacle; relatively unknown actors bringing their (considerable) talents to bear unencumbered by preconceptions; dialogue as it would occur in life, not just words intended solely for the viewer and near enough flashed up as intertitles while the characters choke on schmaltz; in short, the cohesiveness that comes from having one person in charge from the outset, pursuing a distinct editorial vision. As it happens, both movies also fail to stick the landing, but so be it. *Memory Lane* is only sixty-eight minutes long (perhaps it was made with film festivals in mind) and for all that Holmes and co-writer Hari Sathappan concentrated on proofing their script against extraneous material, it's hard not to think they were somewhat more attuned to their own knowledge of the story than how an outsider might perceive it. That doesn't mean the end product is not well worth watching, or that up-and-coming auteurs like Holmes don't deserve awards for kicking down the doors of an industry so corporately skewed it would rather spend $73 million making *Battlefield Earth* than give new writer-directors the time of day. It just means there's even better to come.

To praise any film relative to its funding or that of other productions must surely do it a disservice – *Memory Lane* requires no special consideration to secure its recommendation – but in this instance the figures demand mention, if only because they will seem hard to credit. *Memento* started life with a budget of $4.5 million. *Primer* was brought to the screen for only $7,000. *Memory Lane* cost about $300. It was made (in the sense of remuneration, not skills deployed) as an amateur production: a labour of love. Yet, the core idea and its realisation belie the lack of finances, and either the script was written with certain actors in mind or Holmes has the Midas touch in casting unknowns to fit each part. The cinematography is not always slick (Holmes took responsibility for everything himself), but if anything this rawness adds something to the characters' emotional state and to the immediacy of what's taking place; it certainly doesn't detract, or prevent Holmes from sending us twenty-five years down memory lane, back to when we first saw *Flatliners*.

Since its festival run (and before that, a limited pre-release online) *Memory Lane* has garnered quite some renown as the $300 film. More than that, though, it is an estimable movie in its own right, and the first step – taken without shoes, let alone a shoestring – of a filmmaker who promises to make great strides within the profession. So long as the critical approbation for his debut isn't dependant in some way upon Holmes electrocuting himself in the future, we've much to look forward to.

Jurassic World
Review by Douglas J. Ogurek

Record-breaking, bone-crunching, message-bearing MONSTER of a film.

"No one's impressed by dinosaurs anymore." So says marketing executive Claire (Bryce Dallas Howard) of Jurassic World, a theme park dedicated to giving its visitors the ultimate dinosaur experience. Here visitors navigate glass-enclosed gyrospheres amid brontosauri and triceratops, or get splashed by a gigantic sea creature that eats a shark carcass as if it were a Skittle.

Claire's statement reverberates powerfully in a society whose members are constantly hankering for the newest gadget, the biggest thrill, or, dare I say, the latest blockbuster film. How many of those who helped *Jurassic World*, directed by Colin Trevorrow, claw and tear its way past *The Avengers* (2012) to achieve the highest-grossing opening weekend (US $208.8 million) of all time were lured by the preview featuring that aquatic colossus?

Sure, tons of advertising and the strength of three previous films propelled *Jurassic World*'s box office blitzkrieg, but that doesn't discount the film for what it is: an action-packed adventure and, to the more perceptive, a cautionary tale regarding mankind's unceasing craving to control nature. *Jurassic World* comments on the potentially catastrophic results of our collective quest to get the biggest and the best. By the way, try to see it in IMAX and 3-D.

The Rex Big Thrill
Though the Jurassic World theme park has achieved a ninety-plus percent satisfaction rate, market research reveals its visitors are still looking for the next big thrill. Thus, the scientists in this sprawling, corporation-owned campus cook up a genetically

modified badass of a dinosaur and give it a name wrought with fear (and marketability): Indominus rex! It's bigger and badder than the T-rex. And just imagine that name stretched across a 64-ounce cup of soda!

Of course, Indominus rex escapes.

The rest of the film unfolds entertainingly, if unsurprisingly. When the creature escapes, Claire's nephews get stuck in the park. So she runs to Navy vet Owen (Chris Pratt), a kind of dinosaur trainer stationed on the Jurassic World grounds. Together, the prudish Claire (who never takes off her heels) and the gruff, yet sensitive and sagely Owen – think Patrick Swayze – set out to save the nephews and thwart the beast. The special bond that Owen has developed with four velociraptors (the roving thugs of previous Jurassic Park films) will come into play. Make no mistake: these things are still capable of tearing off Owen's or anyone else's face.

Jurassic World's taut story and jaw-dropping special effects make it a pleasure to watch. However, between the roars, the screams, and the crunching of bones, the film does whisper an important message.

It's About Control

There is a scene about two-thirds into the film – I'm not giving anything major away here – in which a group of commandos approach the island via helicopter. One of them sees a pterodactyl flying peacefully alongside the chopper, blows it away, and then smirks. It's a jarring scene, and it begs further exploration.

Perhaps the bearded gunman is best viewed in light of an earlier, more touching scene in which Claire and Owen comfort a dying brontosaurus. Owen, surveying a landscape littered with dinosaur corpses, makes a conclusion about the escaped Indominus rex: "She's killing for sport." Thus, this destructive creature, made by man, has adapted a very human trait. We need only to look to the barbarian in the helicopter to see it played out.

The theme of *Jurassic World* is best summarised by the word "control", which comes up often. The scientists exercise a fallible control as they Frankenstein the ultimate dinosaur, while Claire controls her perception of the beast as a means to strengthen the bottom line.

However, nobody lives up to the control label more than the chief bad guy Hoskins, played by the ever-cocksure Vincent D'Onofrio. Hoskins, eager to prove his theory that dinosaurs can be the ultimate war machines, repeatedly butts heads with Owen. After the chaos is unleashed, Hoskins stands on a platform overlooking the park and gleefully observes the dinosaur mutiny. What better way to test Hoskins's theory than with Owen's foursome of velociraptors?

Knuckleheaded Love
The romantic tension between Claire and Owen – their one date didn't work out – will appeal to the inevitable knucklehead who needs a side order of love with his or her blockbuster. Claire is the uptight, childless professional. Dressed in a pristine, almost virginal white blouse, skirt, and heels, Claire is the statistic-spouting moneymaker whose soul has been sucked out by the corporation. What better match than the motorcycle-riding Navy vet with a Tarzan-like connection with the beasts? A great pairing on the silver screen. A catastrophe in real life.

Meow Meow MONSTERS!
Dr Henry Wu, Jurassic World's unscrupulous lead scientist, says, "To a mouse, a cat is a monster. We're just used to being the cats." Perhaps this statement best explains *Jurassic World*'s strongest lure: MONSTERS!

The film exploits this fascination from the opening scene, which not only starts with the antagonist (typically a no-no), but also replaces the anticipated cute creature emerging from an egg with a menacing-looking black claw. With apocalyptic fiction all the rage, *Jurassic World* hatches at just the right time, perpetuating the man vs nature mythos.

No one's interested in dinosaurs? Au contraire. *Jurassic World*'s opening weekend has 208.8 million reasons to prove that we most certainly are. ★★★★★

Poltergeist

Review by Douglas J. Ogurek

Rockwell's performance shines in otherwise bland remake.

Advertisements for the *Poltergeist* remake feature a malicious-looking clown, a black background, and the hashtag #WhatAreYouAfraidOf. It looks scary, and it's a smart way to link one of the most enduring images from the 1982 original with contemporary lingo. Too bad strong ads aren't predictors of strong films.

The first *Poltergeist* was a big deal. The supernatural extravaganza struck fear into the hearts of kids and paved the way for many horror films. The 2015 rehash offers a similar storyline embellished with a few technological adornments (to show it's contemporary): a teen texting, iPads, a video drumming game, and even a droid.

Sadly, *Poltergeist*'s resurrection, despite its respect for the original and a competent performance by male lead Sam Rockwell, comes up a bit flimsy. This one isn't going to make it onto many people's #WhatAreYouAfraidOf list, especially when it's compared to recent haunted house films like *Paranormal Activity* (2007), *Insidious* (2010), *The Conjuring* (2013), and *The Babadook* (2014). Even the hyped up clown plays a minuscule role and the preview gives away its chief scare.

After getting laid off, Eric Bowen moves his family to a more affordable Illinois suburb. Unfortunately, the foreclosure-ridden neighborhood sits atop a former Indian burial ground. As the family attempts to settle in, strange things start happening... with toys, trees, electricity, and appliances. Then, you know the words. Come on... sing along! The supernatural entities get angrier, the threats increase, the paranormal investigators show, the family members undertake heroic efforts to save their loved ones. There's the weird little boy, the ball moving on its own, and the stay-at-home mom who has it in her to be a great artist (in this case it's a writer) if only she wasn't tied down by her kids.

The only novel technique this film employs involves flying a drone through the house and into the transdimensional portal. However, it doesn't really add anything to the film.

Most of the film's attempts at humour fall short. I hoped that Jared Harris's take on TV celebrity/ spiritual medium Carrigan Burke would transcend the norm. Alas, plopping an Irish accent on what has become a cookie cutter paranormal investigator doesn't do the trick. One relationship that could have been played up was that between Burke and his nerdy but endearing ex-wife Dr Brooke Powell. The film's funniest scene involves a minor character: a young investigator who loses his drill on the other side of the closet wall as he tries to install a monitoring device. When the spirits on the other side use the young man's drill to "screw" with him, it's hard to keep from laughing.

All's Well with Rockwell

Sam Rockwell all but carries this film. In a genre in which the male lead is often unmemorable at best, Rockwell injects verve and individuality into a character who would be easily forgotten in less capable hands. Eric Bowen, victim of the corporate juggernaut, is down-to-earth and humorous, yet flawed... the kind of guy you'd like as your next-door neighbour. Bowen gives his kids high fives, plays with his wife, eats chicken nugget covered pizza, talks while chewing, and pretends he's getting attacked by a killer squirrel. When the tears well as Bowen says all he wants is for his daughter's safe return, Rockwell is, despite the absurdity of the situation, believable. That's the sign of a good actor.

It's entertaining to watch Bowen's spendthrift leanings exacerbate the guilt he feels for his inability to be a provider. One night, he comes home with gifts for each family member. In one of the film's most

compelling scenes, Bowen tries to make light of the situation when his credit cards don't work at a home improvement store.

One could argue that this film would have been much more interesting if all the supernatural hocus pocus were stripped away and instead it tightened the focus on the familial and financial challenges of this character.

Frightening Doesn't Strike Twice
Ultimately, this movie suffers from the requirement that it must pay homage to a film that made an impact thirty years ago. As time passes, social norms change. What was scary thirty years ago isn't scary today.

One need look no further than the film's most recognised line ("They're here...") to see the degradation that has occurred. The original Carol Anne's utterance is cautionary, yet playful. Carol Anne's 21st century reincarnation Madison treats the line in a way that's best described as dispassionate.

Maybe, for this one, the spirit of the original is best left at rest. ★★★☆☆

Notes

Also Received, But Not Yet Reviewed

Notes by Stephen Theaker

Anderson, Justin Lee, *Carpet Diem*

Downton, Toby, *Solarversia*

Edginton, Ian, and Steve Yeowell, *The Red Seas, Book One: Under the Banner of King Death* (Rebellion): digital-only collection of pirate adventure; looks fun.

Edginton, Ian, and Steve Yeowell, *The Red Seas, Book Two: Fire Across the Deep* (Rebellion)

Hickey, Andrew, *Head of State* (Obverse Books): a novel about Faction Paradox (time-travelling anarchists from the eighth Doctor's run of BBC novels).

Hurley, Andrew Michael, *The Loney* (John Murray)

Langmead, Oliver, *Dark Star* (Unsung Stories)

Magrs, Paul, *The Brenda and Effie Mysteries: Spicy Tea and Sympathy* (Bafflegab Productions): read by Anne Reid, third in the Brenda and Effie series of audios.

Magrs, Paul, *The Brenda and Effie Mysteries: Brenda Has Risen from the Grave* (Bafflegab): starring Anne Reid, Dan Starkey and Stephen Critchlow.

Mayerson, Ginger (ed.), *Storylandia 15: The Julie Travis Collection* (Wapshott Press): a special issue devoted to the work of Julie Travis.

Novik, Naomi, *Uprooted* (Macmillan): comes with a glowing comment from Ursula Le Guin.

Palmer, Stephen, *Beautiful Intelligence* (Infinity Plus Books)

Pratt, Tim, *The Deep Woods* (PS Publishing)

Reynolds, Alastair, *Slow Bullets* (Tachyon Publications)
Watt, D.P., *The Phantasmagorical Imperative and
    Other Fabrications* (The Interlude House)

Forthcoming Attractions

Expect **Theaker's Quarterly Fiction #53** in October
or so. Deadline for submissions is **September 1**.

Our blog isn't at its most active, but it's still there:
www.theakersquarterly.blogspot.com

Stephen tweets every few days or so at:
www.twitter.com/Rolnikov

The zine now has its own Twitter account too:
www.twitter.com/TheakersQrtly

Our email address is:
theakersquarterlyfiction@gmail.com